"I don't think Tia's t        D0616564
Jessica yelled after her, l
and kept going. She didn't want them to see her cry.
But she'd only walked about twenty feet when Ken
rounded the corner and bumped into her.

"Uh, sorry," he said, smiling. "I was just coming to
see you." Maria crossed her arms over her chest and
stared at him.

"I'm exhausted, Ken," she said, hoping he'd take the
hint and leave her alone.

"No problem," Ken said, backing up a little and
holding up his palms. "Look, I know you're upset. I just
wanted you to know that you can talk to me if you
need to. . . . I mean, about your parents."

Maria's whole body tensed. "Is that it?" she asked.

Ken drew back. "Well, actually, I was also going to
ask you if I can get a couple of tickets for Saturday's
performance," he said hesitantly. "So I can . . . come see
you."

Maria closed her eyes and exhaled sharply. "You
know what? Don't even bother coming," she said, holding up one hand. "I'm going to suck, and no one wants
to see me anyway." She turned around and stomped
back down the hall, staring at the floor all the way to
avoid Tia and Jessica. *I don't even know why I came
tonight,* she thought, pushing the dressing-room door
so hard, it knocked against the cement wall before
swinging shut again. *This whole thing is pointless.*

Don't miss any of the books in SWEET VALLEY HIGH
SENIOR YEAR, an exciting new series from Bantam Books!

*Visit the Official Sweet Valley Web Site on the Internet at:*

# http://www.sweetvalley.com

# Francine Pascal's SVH senioryear

# Maria Who?

## CREATED BY
## FRANCINE PASCAL

BANTAM BOOKS
NEW YORK · TORONTO · LONDON · SYDNEY · AUCKLAND

RL 6, age 12 and up

MARIA WHO?

A Bantam Book / September 1999

17th
Street
Productions
A Division of Daniel Weiss Associates, Inc.

Produced by 17th Street Productions,
a division of Daniel Weiss Associates, Inc.
33 West 17th Street
New York, NY 10011.

ISBN: 0-553-49280-2

Published simultaneously in the United States and Canada

Bantam Books are published by Bantam Books, a division of Random
House, Inc. Its trademark, consisting of the words "Bantam Books" and
the portrayal of a rooster, is Registered in U.S. Patent and Trademark
Office and in other countries. Marca Registrada. Bantam Books, 1540
Broadway, New York, New York 10036.

PRINTED IN THE UNITED STATES OF AMERICA

OPM    0 9 8 7 6 5 4 3 2 1

*To Caroline & Ulrika Johansson*

# Maria Slater

In <u>Crime</u> <u>and</u> <u>Punishment,</u> Raskolnikov tries to commit the perfect murder. The problem is, he spends so much time obsessing over his crime that he screws up and gets caught. Same thing in <u>The</u> <u>Tell-Tale</u> <u>Heart.</u> That guy thinks about his victim so much that he goes totally crazy and ends up confessing to the murder even though he's not a serious suspect.

So what do these psychos have to do with my life? Well, I kind of feel like I'm in the same boat as they were. I'm not saying that I've committed some kind of heinous crime or anything, but I'm definitely spending way too much time obsessing over things. And if I keep sitting around here dwelling on all of this Liz-Conner betrayal stuff, I'm going to go completely insane. So I guess there's only one thing to do—I've got to find some way to channel all of this pent-up energy before I self-destruct too.

# Elizabeth Wakefield

I wish I could go back in time—or maybe forward. Anywhere but right now. If I could go back two weeks, Maria would still be my friend, and I'd have a chance to be up front with her about Conner before it blew up in my face. Or if I could go forward a month or so, maybe Conner would be willing to talk to me about his mom's alcoholism instead of hating me for finding out about it. Better yet, if I could skip forward ten years, this whole terrible mess would be nothing but a distant memory. Maybe I'd even be able to laugh about it.

The problem is, I'm stuck here in the present, where my best friend won't talk to me, my "boyfriend" can't forgive me, and I don't have a clue how to make things better. What I wouldn't give for a time machine.

# TIA RAMIREZ

I HONESTLY LOVE ANGEL. REALLY! BUT SOMETIMES IT'S SO HARD KNOWING THAT HE HAS TO LEAVE FOR COLLEGE IN, LIKE, THREE MONTHS. OKAY, SO I KNOW HE'LL COME HOME MOST WEEKENDS AND HAVE LONG BREAKS AND STUFF, AND I KNOW I CAN GO VISIT HIM TOO—WHICH I WILL, EVERY CHANCE I GET. (AS LONG AS I CAN CONVINCE ANDY OR CONNER OR ONE OF MY OTHER CAR-OWNING FRIENDS TO GO ON A ROAD TRIP.) BUT STILL, ONCE ANGEL LEAVES, EVERYTHING WILL BE DIFFERENT. HE WON'T BE ABLE TO JUST SHOW UP ON MY DOORSTEP WHENEVER HE WANTS TO HANG OUT, AND I WON'T BE ABLE TO SWING BY THE GARAGE ON MY WAY HOME FROM SCHOOL TO TALK HIM INTO COMING OVER FOR DINNER OR GOING FOR A WALK OR WHATEVER. AND THEN THERE ARE MY BROTHERS. SOMETIMES I THINK LITTLE TOMÁS IS GOING TO MISS ANGEL MORE THAN I AM!

OKAY, I NEED TO GET A GRIP. IT'S NOT LIKE HE'S LEAVING TOMORROW, OR NEXT WEEK, OR EVEN NEXT MONTH. IF I ADD UP ALL THE NIGHTS AND WEEKENDS LEFT BEFORE HE GOES, THERE'S STILL A LOT OF TIME. WE JUST HAVE TO MAKE EVERY SECOND COUNT.

BESIDES, PEOPLE ALWAYS SAY ABSENCE MAKES THE HEART GROW FONDER, RIGHT? I KEEP REPEATING THAT OVER AND OVER IN MY HEAD, BUT EVERY TIME I GET MYSELF HALFWAY CONVINCED EVERYTHING'S GOING TO BE ALL RIGHT, I THINK ABOUT ANGEL GETTING INVITED TO COLLEGE DANCES AND PARTIES WHERE THE GIRLS WILL BE ALL OVER HIM BECAUSE—LET'S FACE IT—HE'S GORGEOUS. GIRLS HIT ON HIM WHEN I'M STANDING RIGHT THERE, SO WHAT'S GOING TO STOP THEM WHEN I'M A COUPLE HUNDRED MILES AWAY? AND THEN I START THINKING ABOUT THAT OTHER SAYING— OUT OF SIGHT, OUT OF MIND. SOMEHOW I CAN'T HELP THINKING THAT ONE'S MORE TRUTHFUL.

# Angel Desmond

## Estimated College Expenses

Clothes—$350

(socks, boxers, T-shirts, jeans, khakis, etc.)

New running shoes—$85

1st-semester books—$350

Notebooks, pens, paper, calculator, etc.—$150

Minifridge for dorm room—$85

Other stuff—$500

(laundry basket, detergent, towels, sheets, groceries)

Bus fare—???

Total—$1,520

Okay. I'm dead.

# CHAPTER 1

## New Directions

Maria Slater rinsed her orange-juice glass and placed it in the dishwasher. *What I could use now is a hot cup of coffee,* she thought, toying with the idea of heading down to House of Java.

She pictured herself at the counter, ordering a mocha latte and then plopping into one of the cozy, overstuffed chairs by the window to read Jane Austen. *A perfect start to the weekend. Quiet. Relaxing. Surrounded by the sound of rustling newspapers and the smell of freshly ground coffee . . . and a bunch of kids from SVH,* Maria thought, her fantasy coming to an abrupt end. *With my luck Liz and Conner would be there, staring into each other's eyes.*

Maria drummed her fingers on the ivory counter. *But I can't just hang around here avoiding everyone either,* she told herself, rolling her eyes.

"Ugh. I've got to get a life!"

She opened one of the white porcelain canisters on the kitchen counter and scooped out some of the fine brown grounds. Then, pouring cold spring water into the coffeemaker, she flicked on the switch

1

and stood back to listen as the dark liquid began streaming into the glass carafe. *The sound of my day starting,* she thought, musing at what a coffee addict she'd become.

Grabbing her backpack, Maria headed out to the sunroom at the back of her family's house, deciding that one of the wicker chairs her mother had just re-upholstered would be just as comfortable as any chair at House of Java. Her coffee was just as good too, and it wouldn't cost three dollars a cup. Removing her English notebook from her bag, Maria flipped through the pages, searching for her assignment. *Damn. I forgot to write it down again,* she chastised herself.

Automatically she snatched the cordless phone from the table to her left and started to punch in Elizabeth's number. But after three digits she stopped and stared at the receiver, feeling her attempt at a good mood slipping away. She and Elizabeth still weren't talking.

She set down the phone, and it rang, causing Maria to jump. She hit the talk button while trying to calm her racing heart.

"Hello?"

"Hello, could I speak with Maria, please?" The voice sounded vaguely familiar.

"This is Maria," she said.

"Hi, Maria. This is Ms. Delaney. I hate to bother you at home, but if you have a second, there's something I'd like to talk to you about."

"Sure," Maria answered, wondering what she could possibly have done wrong to merit a call from her drama teacher on the weekend.

"You must have heard about the play we're doing this year," Ms. Delaney continued. "*Courting Priscilla?*"

"Yeah," Maria responded. Tia and Jessica had been going to practices every day for over two weeks. It had taken the place of cheerleading as their number-one topic of discussion.

"Well, I'm afraid we've run into a bit of a snag, and I was hoping you could help us out. Our female lead, Renee Talbot, is in the hospital."

"Oh, no," Maria said with a gasp. "I hope she's okay."

"She's fine," Ms. Delaney assured her. "Just a routine appendectomy, but unfortunately she's going to be out of commission for a week or two, and we open this Saturday."

"That's too bad," Maria said, wondering where Ms. Delaney was going with this.

"So," Ms. Delaney said slowly, "I was hoping you could take over her role. I've seen your ability in class, and I think you would be perfect."

Maria almost dropped the phone. She hadn't even auditioned for the play. "*Me?* But I don't even know the part. Isn't there an understudy or something?"

"Not officially, although there are a few girls in

the cast who could probably pull it off. But I'll be honest with you, Maria," Ms. Delaney said, her voice taking on a serious tone. "Quite frankly, none of them possesses even one ounce of your stage presence."

Maria's jaw fell. She nervously twirled a strand of her thick, black hair around one finger. *I can't believe this is happening,* she thought.

"In fact," Ms. Delaney continued, "I can't think of anyone else I'd rather have play Priscilla."

"Uh, I—um," Maria stammered.

"Don't decide now," Ms. Delaney instructed her. "I'll tell you what. There's an afternoon rehearsal today at two-thirty. Go to the library, find a copy of the play, and read through it. Then if you're interested, come to the rehearsal. All you have to do is show up and the part is yours."

"Wow," Maria said, her eyes so wide, she was sure Ms. Delaney could see them over the phone. "All right. I'll look it over."

"Great. I hope to see you later," Ms. Delaney said.

"Yeah . . . bye," Maria responded, slowly replacing the phone in its cradle. For a moment she stood staring out the window at the backyard. "Unbelievable."

Maria walked back to the kitchen and pulled a dark blue mug from one of the cabinets. She shakily poured herself some of the freshly made coffee, added a little milk, and swirled it slowly with a spoon. The very idea of starring in a play after one week of rehearsal was petrifying.

She took a sip of her coffee and leaned back against the butcher-block island in the center of the kitchen.

"But on the other hand . . ."

A playful smile lit Maria's face. She placed her cup on the counter and grabbed a piece of notepaper and a pen from her mother's small desk.

*11 a.m.*

*Mom and Dad,*

*Gone to the library and then possibly to the school for a play rehearsal! (I'll explain when I get home.) Back by 5 p.m.*

*Love,*
*Maria*

Maria propped the slip of paper up against a vase of flowers on the kitchen table and returned to the sunroom. There was one more thing she needed to do before heading to the library.

She picked up the phone and punched in a number, aware that her heart had been beating double time ever since she had spoken with Ms. Delaney. *I'm way too hyped up to make this decision on my own,* she thought. *I definitely need a second opinion.*

"Thanks," Angel said, smiling as he took his coffee from the dark-haired girl at the counter at House of Java. He wound his way through the maze of tables and chairs in the café to the small alcove in the back where Tia, Andy, and Conner were sitting. He was just in time to catch the end of their conversation.

"I'm just saying you should think about it," Tia said, removing the barrette she had clenched between her teeth and clipping her long, brown hair into a loose ponytail. "'Cause if you ask me, you really screwed up this time."

Angel smirked as he slid into the free chair next to his girlfriend. Tia's brown eyes were sparkling, the way they always did when she was giving someone her unabashed opinion. He loved that Tia was so direct. It meant that he never had to waste time wondering how she really felt about things.

"Can't we go ten minutes without talking about *her?*" Conner snapped, his green eyes flashing and his jaw visibly clenched. Tia had obviously brought up the Conner-unfriendly topic of Elizabeth Wakefield. Angel smiled at Tia weakly, mentally urging her to drop the subject. Conner was definitely not in the mood. Tia sighed in defeat, grabbed a spoon from the table, and turned her attention to her coffee. Andy just shrugged and rolled his eyes.

*Tough crowd,* Angel thought, passing one hand over his closely cropped black hair. He took a quick sip of his French roast and then clasped his hands, pointing forward with both index fingers.

"Hey, I've got some good news," he offered, trying to sound upbeat. Tia stopped stirring her coffee and looked up. Conner even blinked in his direction.

"What's up?" Andy asked with a slight nod. "You and Tia finally tying the knot?"

Tia laughed. "Yeah, right. And I'm going to drop out of high school so I can stay home and take care of little Angel," she finished, patting her stomach.

"Hey, being married wouldn't be such a bad thing, baby," Angel said, grinning down at her. "I think *Angel Junior* sounds kind of cool."

Tia raised one eyebrow. "Sorry to burst your bubble," she returned, "but I don't plan to squeeze out any *niños* for a *long* time. I've three little brothers, remember? It'll be *at least* ten years before I even think about having any of my own." She paused to look up at Angel coyly. "But I could marry you in five, if you're still interested."

"Absolutely," Angel said, draping his arm around her neck and pulling her closer. "That'll give me just enough time to save up for the incredible honeymoon you deserve." Tia squeezed Angel's arm, and he nuzzled his nose into her thick, dark brown hair, inhaling the subtle scent of her coconut shampoo.

"Enough already," Andy said, grabbing the back of Angel's denim shirt and pulling him away from Tia.

"Whoa! Since when do you have the strength of ten men?" Angel asked, shaking himself free of Andy's grip and straightening his button-down shirt. At five-foot nothing and one hundred and nothing, Andy was better known for his curly red hair than his brawn.

"Ever since you and Juliet here started reenacting the balcony scene," Andy shot back. "See, whenever people start to act nauseatingly cute, my adrenaline gets pumping and I react like I'm in the middle of a crisis," he added in a perfect deadpan, earning a chuckle from Conner.

"So anyway," Andy continued, looking at Angel. "You said you had some good news . . . ," he prodded.

"That's right," Angel said, straightening up in his chair. "You know how the Riot's had that Help Wanted sign up for eons?" He paused just long enough for them to nod. "Well, you happen to be sitting with their new bartender." Angel looked around the table for reactions, but Conner and Andy clammed up. They were both staring at Tia.

"Excuse me?" Tia said, glowering at Angel. "When did this happen? And what about the garage?

Are you telling me you're going to be working *two* jobs now? Because I know you don't have time for that—"

Angel held up his hand. "Hold on a second, baby. Let me explain." He had hoped that breaking the news to her in front of Conner and Andy would temper her reaction a little, but he should have known better.

"I'm gonna get another coffee," Andy said, standing up. "You coming, Conner?"

"Yeah," Conner responded, flashing Angel a sympathetic look and following Andy to the counter.

*Traitors,* Angel thought.

"Well?" Tia said, commanding his attention. Angel gazed back at her blankly, unsure where to start.

"When did this happen anyway?" Tia asked. "I left you last night at midnight, and it's not even noon," she added, checking her watch. "So either you've been real busy for the last twelve hours, or—"

"I know where you're going," Angel responded quickly, "but I haven't been keeping this from you. I just got the job this morning," he said, looking directly into Tia's large brown eyes. "Honest. I stopped by the Riot on my way here."

Tia exhaled sharply. "Why?" she asked, beginning to look more hurt than angry. "You already have a job."

"That's just it," Angel responded. "I've been

9

working like crazy at the garage, but you'd never know it from looking at my bank account. I've barely got enough to last me through the first couple of weeks at school. And when I come home to visit you, I won't have any money to do anything."

"We don't have to spend money to have fun," Tia said, fluttering her lashes.

Angel gently pushed a stray strand of hair behind her ear. "I'm serious, Tee. At this point I can't afford to drive five extra miles. So even if you just want to take a walk on the beach, we still have to get there and back, and that's five dollars of gas money that I don't have."

Tia looked down at her lap, and Angel steeled himself, anticipating another round of questions. But instead she reached out for Angel's hand and took it in her own. "I'm sorry, Angel. I know I'm half the reason you're working so hard," she said, pulling his hand to her lips and giving it a quick kiss. "It's just that—" Tia paused to look into Angel's eyes. "Well, why did you have to run out and get *another* job? I mean, can't your dad just up your hours or give you a raise or something?"

Angel observed the hopeful look in Tia's eyes. "I wish it were that easy, Tee, but it's not. Forty hours is as high as he can go right now—I asked." Tia slouched in her chair as if his words had deflated her. "Believe me," he continued, squeezing her hand, "I tried to come up with something else, but taking another job is the only way I'm ever going to get enough money saved up for college. Especially since I only have a few months left."

Tia rolled her eyes. "Oh, great, another one of my favorite topics," she said.

"Come on, Tee," Angel pleaded. "The more I save, the more I can come back to see you on weekends. But I've got to have the money if I'm going to come back at all."

Tia's features softened. "I know," she said reluctantly. "I just don't like the idea of having even *less* time to spend with you."

Angel leaned in and put his arms around Tia. "Baby, I'm going to spend every free second I have with you." Tia smiled up at him. "Besides, I'll be working at your favorite club. You can visit me anytime, and it'll be like we're hanging out together. I'll just have to mix drinks and wipe down a few tables every once in a while."

Tia leaned back to look at Angel, her face brighter now. "That's true. I hadn't thought of it that way. Maybe we can sneak up to the roof on your breaks," she suggested, raising her eyebrows.

Angel beamed back at her. "Thanks for understanding, Tee," he said. "You're the best." He heaved a sigh of relief as Tia flashed him a grin.

"Yes, I am," she agreed. "And we're going to get that tattooed across your forehead before you leave for college so you don't ever forget it."

\*     \*     \*

Ken Matthews jogged up the wide granite steps to the Sweet Valley Public Library and swung open one of the heavy wooden doors. He didn't mind hanging out in the library every once in a while, but he always found the atmosphere a little intimidating when he first entered—especially the way all the street noise came to an abrupt halt as soon as the enormous door had closed behind him.

*Why would Maria want me to meet her here?* he wondered as he walked across the brown-carpeted entryway and headed left into the literature section. *I hope everything's all right.* Ken walked past row after row of books until he came to an open area spotted with round tables.

Maria was sitting alone in the center. She looked okay. She was wearing one of her most worn outfits, a snug, long-sleeved, black T-shirt over army green cargo pants. But then he noticed the way her leg was bouncing uncontrollably under the table and the fact that her thick black hair was shooting out in seventeen different directions—an obvious result of having combed her hands through it countless times. She was flipping hurriedly through a paperback, her eyes darting across the pages.

Maria was tense.

Ken frowned and quickly crossed the room. "Hey," he said, pulling out a chair at the table and sitting down. "What's going on?"

Maria looked up, startled. "Oh, Ken, I didn't even see you come in. Thanks for meeting me."

"No problem," Ken said, narrowing his blue eyes. "So what's this thing you wanted to run by me?"

Maria flashed him a big smile, her eyes sparkling. "You're not going to believe this," she said. Ken couldn't help smiling back at her. Whether Maria was unusually psyched or unusually irate, she had a way of sucking Ken in.

"So what happened?" he asked.

"Okay," Maria continued, taking a deep breath. "Ms. Delaney called this morning and told me Renee Talbot—who's supposed to play the lead in the play this weekend—is in the hospital." Ken furrowed his eyebrows. "She's all right and everything," Maria added quickly, "but she had her appendix out, so she's not going to be able to do the play."

"That's too bad," Ken said. "Are you guys friends?"

"No," Maria answered, shaking her head. "I barely know her." She ran one hand through her thick hair, causing it to stand up even more. "The unbelievable part is that Ms. Delaney wants *me* to take over the role for Renee, and I didn't even audition for the play in the first place! She just saw me in drama class, and she said she thought I'd be perfect for the part."

"That's great," Ken said, beginning to smile. "So are you going to do it?"

Maria squinted thoughtfully. "I'm not sure yet. That's what I wanted to talk to you about. What do you think I should do?"

"Me?" Ken asked, dumbfounded. "Uh, I don't know, Maria. I mean, isn't this something you should decide for yourself?"

"I guess," Maria answered reluctantly. "It's just that lately I seem to be jumping into things without seeing the big picture, and I'm not so sure I can be objective about this on my own."

Ken nodded. He knew that finding out about Conner and Elizabeth had really thrown her. No wonder she didn't trust her instincts right now. Still, he wasn't sure why she had called him, of all people. *Like I should be giving anyone advice,* he thought.

"Is that the play?" he asked, gesturing at the book in Maria's hand.

"Yes, and I absolutely love it," Maria said, hugging it to her chest. "I've scanned most of it, and Priscilla—the character Ms. Delaney wants me to play—is totally cool. She's strong, she's witty, and she's got *at-ti-tude.*" Maria shifted her head from side to side as she slowly pronounced the word. "But she's also vulnerable, which makes her believable. It would be a great role, not to mention the fact that there's an excellent plot and the rest of the characters are interesting too." Maria bit her lip in an unsuccessful attempt to hide her excitement.

"That sounds like a pretty strong vote for doing

the play," Ken said. "Are there any reasons for *not* doing it?"

Maria took another deep breath and held it for a moment before exhaling. "Well, I don't usually like to do school plays because everyone gets all catty and competitive when they're trying out for roles and everything."

"But the auditions are over, right?" Ken asked.

"Yeah," Maria admitted. "And the cast has been working together for weeks now, so they've probably worked out most of the kinks too. But then there's the fact that the play opens in a week. That's just seven days to get into the character, learn all my lines, find my marks, and rehearse." She looked at Ken doubtfully. "That's almost impossible," she added, shifting her gaze to the ceiling and shaking her head slightly.

"*Almost* impossible," Ken repeated. "You acted as a kid, right?"

"Yeah," Maria answered, "but that was a long time ago."

Ken nodded. "I know, but you've got a lot of experience with this stuff. So can you do it all in a week?"

Maria knitted her brow. "Yeah," she said. "It'd be tough, but I think I can do it."

Ken could tell Maria was really excited about this. She just needed a little push. "Okay, so what *other* reasons do you have for not doing it?" he asked.

Maria looked at him shyly, barely meeting his eyes. "I'm kind of nervous," she confided. "What if I'm not any good?"

Ken leaned in closer so that Maria had to look at him. "Give your drama teacher a little credit. Why do you think she called you?" he said, looking directly into her dark eyes. "There must be lots of people who tried out who could do it, but she must think you have something none of them have."

Maria blushed and looked away.

"Besides," he added, "what's the worst that could happen?"

Maria glanced at him from the corner of her eye. "I could suck," she answered in a somber voice.

"Nah, Ms. Delaney wouldn't let you go on if you really sucked," Ken said, leaning back in his chair. "She's an *über*director. She'd wheel Renee in on a hospital bed and make her do it."

Maria laughed, touching Ken's arm giddily.

Ken smiled back at her, aware of the warmth her hand was radiating on his forearm. It had been a long time since anyone had touched him in such a casual, friendly way. Their eyes locked for a split second. Then Maria glanced at her watch and quickly stood up to gather her belongings.

"I've got to get out of here if I'm going to make the rehearsal," she said, slinging her bag over her shoulder. She leaned in and gave Ken a quick peck on the cheek. "Thanks so much for talking me through this," she said, straightening up. "You're a lifesaver."

"Anytime," Ken said, his voice a bit raspy. He cleared his throat and shifted in his seat, trying to hide the blush he was certain had taken over his face after Maria had kissed him. She drew her hand across his back and patted his shoulder lightly as she walked past him, causing one more slight twitch.

Ken took a deep breath and let it out slowly, slumping down slightly in his chair. *Get a grip, man,* he told himself. *People touch other people all the time.* And it was just Maria. It was no big deal. She was just a friend.

"So do you think anyone's upset that Maria got the part?" Tia whispered, leaning over the armrest that divided her seat from Jessica's in the first row of the auditorium.

"I don't know," Jessica replied softly, tucking a strand of shoulder-length blond hair behind her ear. "It's kind of annoying since she didn't try out and everything, but I wouldn't want to try to learn it now." She glanced sideways at Tia. "Why? Would you?"

"Are you kidding?" Tia scoffed. "Too much work."

"Cut!" Ms. Delaney yelled, her voice echoing through the cavernous auditorium. It was so loud that Tia snapped to attention even though she realized the

17

director was addressing the actors onstage and not her. "Remember," Ms. Delaney continued, removing her horn-rimmed glasses from her nose and letting them dangle from the beaded strap around her neck, "Bill may be acting like a jerk, but somewhere deep inside, Priscilla's still drawn to him—even if she doesn't recognize it yet." She tapped her chest with her fist, as she always did when she was talking about a character's internal motivation.

Tia watched as Maria nodded slowly, appearing to take in every word the director was saying.

"You should be angry with him, but not detached," Ms. Delaney continued, pushing a strand of wild, salt-and-pepper hair out of her face. She perpetually wore her hair twisted in a loose bun, but there were always stray pieces hanging down around her face—a result of the animated gestures that made Tia refer to her as the drama queen. "There has to be tension between the two of you so the audience will understand where the passion comes from later," Ms. Delaney finished. "Got it?"

This time Maria nodded with more certainty. "Yeah, that makes sense," she said.

"Okay," called Ms. Delaney, clapping. "Places, everyone. Let's take it from Bill's entrance on page eight." Tia watched as the various cast members shuffled back to their places, and Ms. Delaney gave them the signal to begin with a flourish of her hand.

"Hey, how long till you come in?" Tia whispered,

leaning close to Jessica again. Jessica flipped through her script. "Twelve more pages," she answered in a low voice. "I make my grand entrance in *'scene three—at the diner.'*"

Tia almost giggled at Jessica's overly dramatic pronunciation, but she managed to keep quiet.

"That's ridiculous, Bill. I'm not upset," Maria said in the taut voice she had already developed for her character, Priscilla.

"Are you sure?" asked Charlie Rucker, who was playing Bill. "Because the minute I mentioned Laura, you seemed to tense up." He took a step closer to Maria, who was seated at a desk in what was supposed to be Priscilla's office.

"I'm positive," said Maria with a forced smile. "Now why don't you go take care of your *client,* or whatever she is," she continued through clenched teeth. "I have work to do." With that, she looked back down at her desk and began shuffling through papers.

"All right," said Charlie hesitantly, backing toward stage right. "As long as you're sure you're not upset."

"I'm not upset," Maria repeated tersely without looking up. Charlie nodded and exited the stage. As soon as he was gone, Maria stood and wadded up a piece of paper from her desk. "I'm furious!" she yelled, hurling the paper across the stage. Tia and Jessica jumped in their seats.

"Oooh, she's good," Tia whispered, flipping her hair back over her shoulder. "I don't think she's even reading her lines anymore. It's like she memorized the entire scene in twenty minutes."

"Yeah, it's pretty amazing," Jessica agreed, pulling her blue cardigan around her shoulders and sinking further down in her seat. "She's so much better than Renee."

"Renee never threw anything at Charlie," Tia said, raising her index finger. "That was good."

She reached over and grabbed a chip from the small bag Jessica had smuggled in. "You shouldn't be eating in here, you know," she said as she shoved the potato chip in her mouth.

"You know I only bring them in for you," Jessica replied sarcastically.

Tia giggled quietly. "What kind are these anyway? They're spicy," she said.

"Red pepper barbecue," Jessica answered, licking her lips.

"Aren't you worried about your breath?" Tia asked. "You know, for your big kiss with Charlie?"

"Oh, that," Jessica said, waving her salt-covered hand. "We're not rehearsing the kiss until Monday's practice, and trust me, I'll be prepared. I always carry breath mints." She tapped her bag with a grin. "But I do kind of wish we were practicing it today."

"Really?" Tia asked, shooting her friend a sideways glance.

"I didn't mean it that way," Jessica said with a scowl. "It's just that the play's only a week away, and we haven't even practiced kissing yet."

"And just how many times do you think you need to practice it?" Tia asked.

"Come on, Tia," Jessica said, rolling her eyes. "I just mean that I'm a little nervous about it. It's not like I've ever fake-kissed someone in front of an audience before. I don't want it to look all awkward and stuff."

"Yeah, yeah," Tia said. "And I suppose the fact that Charlie Rucker is drop-dead gorgeous has nothing to do with it?"

Jessica blushed slightly. "Well . . . it doesn't hurt. If I have to kiss someone, it might as well be someone cute. Right?"

Tia just shrugged.

"Besides," Jessica continued, "I have a boyfriend."

"And how does he feel about you kissing someone else?" Tia prodded.

"Well, I haven't exactly mentioned it to him yet," Jessica admitted. Tia's eyebrows shot up. "But I'm pretty sure he wouldn't care. Jeremy's not the jealous type, and he'd understand that it's just part of the play. What about Angel?"

"Actually, I asked him about it last night, and he said he's fine with you kissing Charlie," Tia answered matter-of-factly.

Jessica shook her head. "You're such a loser," she

whispered. "I mean, how would Angel feel if you had to kiss another guy?"

"Oh!" Tia said, laughing and hitting her forehead with the heel of her hand. "He wouldn't care. Angel's cool about stuff like that. Then again, we've been together for three years now. If he's not secure in this relationship now, he's never gonna be."

Ms. Delaney called a five-minute break. Maria jogged over and took a seat at Tia's side.

"This is *so* fun," she said, beaming. "Ms. Delaney's a great director, and the cast is so good. I just hope I don't bring the whole production down."

Tia was amazed. "Are you serious?" she asked. Maria hesitated, and Tia could see that she really was concerned about how she was doing.

"You've got to be kidding, Maria," Jessica jumped in. "You're like a teenage Meryl Streep. No one would ever know this is your first day of rehearsal."

"Seriously," Tia added. "You are *totally* Priscilla." Then she leaned in closer and whispered, "No offense to Renee or anything, but you're already way better than she ever was." Jessica nodded.

Maria fell back in her seat. "Thanks, guys, but I'm sure Renee would do a better job. At least she knows the part. I just hope I can get all the lines memorized by Saturday night."

"Don't worry about it," Tia assured her. "It's like you learned the first scene by osmosis or something.

Besides, Jess and I could always help you practice." Maria raised her eyebrows at Jessica, who glanced at Tia, obviously taken off guard by the offer.

Maria shook her head. "That's okay. I don't want to bother you guys with extra rehearsal time. I'm the one who needs it—not you."

Tia exhaled sharply. "Please," she said. "Jessica needs all the help she can get."

"I do believe it was you stumbling over your lines earlier, Tee," Jessica said simply. Then she turned to Maria. "I'm up for extra rehearsal. It could be fun."

Maria looked back and forth between Tia and Jessica, biting her lip, and then she smiled. "That would be great," she answered. "You guys are the best."

"We keep telling everybody that, but no one else seems to believe us," Tia said dryly.

"Go figure," Jessica added with mock astonishment. Maria laughed.

"Hey, speaking of getting together," Tia said, her eyes lighting up, "anybody up for the Riot tonight? It's Angel's first night tending bar."

They didn't even have to answer. Tia knew they were both going to turn her down by the looks in their eyes.

"I'd love to," Jessica said, "but I really think I need to stay home with Liz tonight. She's still moping about Conner."

"I can't believe he still refuses to talk to her," Tia

said, grimacing. "You know what? You should make her come too. She needs to get out of there."

Jessica shook her head. "I don't think she's ready for that," she said. "Besides, I wouldn't want to risk her bumping into Conner. She'd totally freak."

Tia felt Maria start to shift uncomfortably at the Conner-Elizabeth talk. "How about you, Maria?" she asked, trying to keep the mood light.

"I can't," Maria said. "I've got to start memorizing these lines right away if I'm gonna be ready in time. Sorry."

"That's okay," Tia answered, although in truth she was bummed. She was already getting a bad feeling about this second-job stuff, and she had hoped that having a few friends along might help her keep a more positive attitude.

*Oh, well,* she thought as the break came to an end and people started taking their places for the next scene. *I can always see if the guys want to hang out and watch my boyfriend work.*

*How exciting.*

# TIA RAMIREZ

**From:** tee@swiftnet.com
**To:** mcdermott@cal.rr.com,
            marsden1@swiftnet.com
**Time:** 5:07 P.M.
**Subject:** to riot, or not to riot?

hey, boys—
   how about spending an exciting night
watching the love of my life pour drinks?
   (yes, i'm serious, andy, so don't
even bother with the wiseass remarks.)
   riot, 8:30-ish, at the bar. and before you turn me down, remember all of
the lame events i've gone to for both
of you. besides, i know neither one of
you has anything better to do.
   let me know,
                     —tee

# Conner McDermott

**From:** mcdermott@cal.rr.com
**To:** tee@swiftnet.com
**Time:** 5:49 P.M.
**Subject:** re: to riot, or not to riot?

Tee,

I can probably meet you around nine, but if anyone so much as mentions Elizabeth Wakefield—or being awake, or walking through fields, or any other thinly veiled attempts to work her name into the conversation, I'm outta there.

—C.

# Andy Marsden

**From:** marsden1@swiftnet.com
**To:** tee@swiftnet.com
**Time:** 5:58 P.M.
**Subject:** re: to riot, or not to riot?

Tia,

   I'm shocked! Me? A wiseass response? How could you even think such a thing? Especially since watching Angel pour drinks is one of my favorite pastimes. It's right up there with watching earthworms tunnel through the mud and catching Mr. Schneider cleaning out his earwax during math class.

   But yes, I'll be there—in spite of your insensitive remark.

   With the utmost sincerity,

                    Andy ;-)

# CHAPTER 2

AS GOOD AS IT GETS

Jessica shuddered as she turned the cold brass door-knob at the front entrance to the Fowlers' mansion. *I hope our house gets rebuilt soon,* she thought. *I don't know how many more nights I can handle in this tomb.* As she stepped into the enormous foyer and took in the familiar sights of the winding, stucco staircase and the red, ceramic-tile floor, Jessica sighed and shook her head.

Before the earthquake had destroyed the Wakefields' home and long before she and Lila had ceased to be friends, Jessica used to dream of own-ing a house as magnificent as this one. But after hav-ing lived there for a couple of months, Jessica had realized that the comfort of the Wakefields' cozy, split-level ranch was much more her style.

*And here comes half the reason why,* Jessica thought, hearing familiar footsteps plodding toward the foyer.

"Miss Wakefield," Mrs. Pervis called.

Jessica groaned softly, wondering what she'd done wrong now. She turned to face the stout housekeeper and forced herself to smile. "Hello, Mrs. Pervis. How are you today?" she asked, trying to sound sincere.

"A parcel arrived for you while you were out, Miss Wakefield," Mrs. Pervis said.

"A package? For me?" Jessica asked, her eyes widening. Mrs. Pervis gestured toward the large table where she sorted and placed the Fowlers' mail each day, and sure enough, right in the center there was a rectangular package wrapped in plain, brown paper.

Jessica walked quickly over to it, excited to see where it was from, but there was no return address. In fact, as she turned the box over in her hands, she realized her address hadn't even been written on it— just her name, in cutout magazine letters.

"Oh, great," she said, flashing back to all the cruel pranks Melissa Fox had pulled. Gingerly she lifted the box to her ear and shook it gently. *At least it's not ticking*, she thought sarcastically, setting it back down.

"I wonder what it is," she muttered aloud, staring at the box.

Mrs. Pervis took a step closer, her loose-fitting, long black dress and white apron rustling.

"Whatever the contents," Mrs. Pervis began in a disapproving tone, "you might encourage your friends to use the postal system like everyone else rather than simply dropping parcels on the stoop.

30

Miss Lila nearly tripped on the package on her way to her tennis lesson this morning."

*Next time I'll make sure it's a larger package so that Lila won't miss,* Jessica mused. "Thank you for the advice," she said sweetly.

At that moment Lila walked into the foyer, dressed in linen pants and an undoubtedly new silk tank top. Jessica locked eyes with her and wondered if Lila would say anything. It had been weeks since they'd spoken to each other.

"Jess," Lila said in chilly acknowledgment, flicking her gaze over the package in Jessica's hands.

"Li," Jessica returned, stiffening.

Lila hovered for a moment longer as if she had something to say, but then changed her mind and headed up the stairs noiselessly.

"Freak," Jessica said under her breath.

Mrs. Pervis narrowed her eyes, but Jessica just smiled innocently and tore off the brown paper to expose a plain, gold box. It didn't look threatening. She opened the lid and folded back two pieces of white tissue paper, revealing a black leather book.

"That's weird," she said. "Who would be sending me an anonymous book?"

Jessica lifted it from the box and ran her hand over the cover. The pages were gilded with gold edging, and a red silk ribbon hung loosely from the top of the binding. As Jessica flipped through it, she realized it wasn't a book at all, but a journal. *It's perfect,*

31

she thought, admiring the thick, textured paper. *And I need a new one.* She thumbed through the pages again, hoping to find a card or a note, but there was nothing. Still, Jessica was fairly certain she knew who had left it.

She couldn't wait for her morning shift at House of Java so she could thank Jeremy in person. Jessica closed her eyes and pictured herself running around the counter to hug Jeremy first thing in the morning. She could see his gorgeous brown eyes, and she could almost feel his strong arms wrapping tightly around her.

Jessica was about to go upstairs to make her first journal entry when she saw Elizabeth making her way slowly down the hall toward the top of the staircase. It was nearly six o'clock, but she was still in her bathrobe, and from the looks of her tousled hair, she had spent most of the day lying in bed.

Quickly Jessica stuffed the new journal into her duffel bag. The last thing Elizabeth needed was to have Jessica's romantic gift shoved in her face.

"Hey, Lizzie," Jessica called, starting up the stairs. Elizabeth stared back at her blankly. "That new movie you've been wanting to see is at the Cineplex tonight," Jessica said. "I thought maybe we could go—just the two of us. It's been a while since we've had a sisters' night out." Elizabeth just stared. *Unless it's more fun being catatonic,* Jessica thought.

"What movie?" Elizabeth said, her voice slow and

weak. It was obvious she'd been crying all day.

Jessica cleared her throat. "You know, the one where the girl goes back to her old high school undercover," she prompted, unable to come up with the name.

Elizabeth furrowed her brow for a moment before a look of recognition settled into her eyes. She opened her mouth to speak, but no words came out. Instead she looked like she was ready to start crying again.

"Liz?" Jessica asked, gingerly touching her sister's shoulder. "What is it? What's wrong?"

"I was going to talk Conner into seeing that with me," Elizabeth said quietly. "Of course, that was before he chucked me out of his house."

*Oh, boy,* Jessica thought, pulling Elizabeth close and hugging her while she sobbed. *This is going to be a long night.*

"Mom? Dad?" Maria called as she rushed through the front door of her house. She had started running at the driveway when she saw that her parents' car was parked in the garage. As she burst into the living room, she was happy to find them together for her big announcement. Her father was lying down on the large, cream-colored sofa, reading the newspaper, and her mother was curled up at the other end, flipping through a home magazine.

"What is it, Maria?" Frances Slater asked, looking up at her daughter. "Is everything all right?"

"Everything's great!" Maria responded as her father folded his paper and sat up to look at her.

"Do you want to hear about my *play rehearsal?*" Maria asked, smiling mischievously.

Jack Slater raised his eyebrows. "We were wondering about that note," he said. "When did you get involved in a play?" Mrs. Slater set her magazine next to the fresh-cut flowers on the pine coffee table and leaned forward.

"This morning," Maria answered, beaming. "It was the strangest thing. Ms. Delaney—you know, my drama teacher?" Her parents nodded. "Well, she called me just a few minutes after you guys left this morning and asked me to take the lead in the school play."

Mrs. Slater gasped. "That's wonderful, dear!" she exclaimed, standing up with outstretched arms to hug her daughter. Maria walked around the coffee table to embrace her mother, then took a seat in one of the matching overstuffed chairs opposite the sofa. Her mother sat down gracefully, tucking the skirt of her long, orange-and-pink batik dress underneath her legs.

"I didn't even know you had auditioned for a play," Mrs. Slater said.

"That's the weird part," Maria answered, clasping her hands in front of her. "I didn't."

"Then how . . . ," her father began, his voice trailing off.

"See, Renee Talbot was supposed to be the lead, but she can't do it because she just had her appendix out," Maria explained, all the words tumbling out in one breath. "So Ms. Delaney called and asked me to take the role. She said she's been watching me in drama class and she thought I'd be perfect for it."

"That's too bad for Renee," Mrs. Slater said, her face sympathetic, "but how wonderful for you, dear."

"Yeah, I'm pretty psyched," Maria said, beaming.

"And I'm sure Ms. Delaney is right about you being perfect for the part," Mrs. Slater continued, smiling at her daughter. "You've always been a wonderful actress."

Maria's giddy grin was uncontrollable. "Thanks, Mom," she said, her eyes sparkling.

"Absolutely," her father added. "Your sister may have gotten the academic ability, but there's nothing wrong with being a performer."

Maria's breath caught in her throat, and her shoulders tensed.

"Nothing at all," her mother said. "Not everyone can expect to go to Brown like Nina. . . ."

"So, it's good to know you have your strengths too," Mr. Slater finished, driving a nail through Maria's heart.

"Oh, we should call Nina," Mrs. Slater said. "She'll

be so happy for you. She's always very gracious and proud of her little sister's achievements."

*Oh, yes! Let's call Miss Perfect. That's what's important. That's what's always important,* Maria thought, glancing at her sister's picture on the mantel. It was twice the size of the dinky picture they had up there of Maria. Her mom had told her it was Nina's senior picture, and they'd order a large one of Maria when she had them taken. But the explanation didn't make the physical evidence any less annoying. *And what does he mean when he says* Nina *got the academic ability? Don't they realize I'm in line for valedictorian and all my teachers practically worship me?*

Maria looked at her mother.

"Are you all right, dear?" Mrs. Slater asked, her eyebrows raised. "Oh! I shouldn't have brought up academics. Are you worried your schoolwork might suffer because of the play?"

Maria forced herself to smile. "No, Mom. I'll be fine. I guess I'm just a little overwhelmed. The play is next Saturday."

"Next Saturday?" her parents said in unison, looking at each other.

"I know," Maria said. "That only gives me seven days to get my lines down—not to mention developing the character and everything else that goes along with being in a play." She looked down at her hands and started picking at her nails. "I just hope I haven't gotten myself in over my head."

Mrs. Slater stood up and walked over to Maria's chair. Bumping Maria over slightly with her hip, she sat down on the edge of the seat and put one arm around Maria. She gently pressed her smooth face against Maria's cheek. Maria took in her mother's fresh, powdery fragrance. It was a combination of rose-scented skin cream and the delicate smells of the extravagant pastries her mother had been baking for local restaurants and cafés ever since Maria had entered high school. Always comforting.

"There's no doubt in my mind that you will be wonderful," Mrs. Slater said softly, pulling back far enough to look straight into her daughter's eyes. Maria smiled.

"And I've been waiting for years to see you back onstage again," her father said from across the room.

Maria gave her mother a squeeze and looked at her father. As a financial analyst, Jack Slater was cool, calculating, and concise, and at six-four and two-hundred-plus pounds, he was an intimidating figure. But as Maria observed the tender smile on his face and the sincere concern in his eyes, she was reminded once again that behind the stoic facade and the booming voice, he was just a big teddy bear.

"You guys really think I'll be okay? Even with only a week to rehearse?" she asked warily.

"Absolutely," her mother said. "And we can't wait to see you." Maria smiled at her parents, grateful for

37

their faith in her and pleased to feel like she'd done something to make them proud.

*And maybe when they see the play,* she thought, *they'll be so proud of me that just for a moment, they'll forget all about Nina.*

"Brace yourself, Tee," Andy said, raising his eyebrows and looking over Tia's left shoulder. "The biggest hair I've ever seen just walked through the door."

They were sitting on adjacent stools at the corner of the bar on the Riot's first floor, ideally positioned for people watching. From her seat Tia had a perfect view of the back half of the room, and Andy could see the dance floor and the entrance.

"Male or female?" Tia inquired, keeping her eyes trained on the two thin, brown stripes across the chest of Andy's oversized, tan camp shirt.

Andy sat up straight and craned his neck a little. Tia watched as he scrutinized the target. "I'm not sure," he said slowly, narrowing his eyes.

"Poor thing." Tia giggled. "Coming this way?" she asked. She had to grip the bar to resist the urge to turn around and gawk.

Andy nodded. "Oh, yeah," he said, reaching to grab a tortilla chip from the basket in front of them. Tia waited patiently for the play-by-play that she knew was coming.

"All right," Andy said, dipping his chip in the

salsa and taking a bite. "She—or he," he corrected himself, causing Tia to giggle again, "has finished looking around the room and is just about to cross the dance floor. Looks like it's headed for the bar."

"It?" Tia asked incredulously. "Now you're just being cruel," she told him, pursing her lips.

Andy scowled. "Whatever," he said, slouching a little and staring down at the bar. "Just get ready to look to your right—I think it's going to order a drink."

Tia reached up and rubbed the back of her neck with her left hand, turning her head to the right nonchalantly. "Yikes," she whispered, turning back to Andy, who laughed into his soda. "Now, that's scary. Do you think it knows that the head-bangers' ball was over ten years ago?"

"Oh—who's being cruel now?" Andy asked.

"Just following your lead," Tia said devilishly, taking a long sip of her soda. "Okay," she said, stirring the ice in her glass with her straw, "we've seen the queen of spandex, that lounge-lizard guy, and Madame le Big Hair over there. You know what I'd like to see now?"

Andy chewed on his bottom lip and studied Tia's face. "A man dressed as a woman dressed as a man?" he guessed.

"No," Tia said, glaring at him. "My boyfriend!"

"Oh, yeah, that guy," Andy said, looking around the bar area.

"Where is he anyway?" Tia said. "We've been here for over an hour, and I've barely had a chance to say two words to him. This new tank top is totally going to waste." Tia adjusted the pale pink straps on her shoulders and pushed the salsa around in its bowl with one of the chips. "And now it's like—poof!— he's gone," she added, throwing one arm wildly into the air.

"Hey—do you guys need anything right now?" Angel's voice came so suddenly, it made Tia jump. She glanced up at Angel and then looked quickly over at Andy, her eyes wide. Andy answered her panicked look with a quick shake of his head, and Tia knew that Angel hadn't been standing there long enough to hear her bitching about him. She let out a big sigh.

"A little time with my boyfriend would be nice," Tia said, smiling up at him. Then she stood up on her footrest and gave him a quick kiss. She felt Angel's body go rigid as he looked quickly over both of his shoulders.

"That's sweet, baby, but I wanted to know if either of you wanted another drink or more chips or anything." Angel paused and looked at Tia and then at Andy.

"Well, look at you, all business," Tia said, a slight edge to her voice.

"I could use another—," Andy started, holding up his empty soda glass.

"What's going on?" Tia interrupted, giving Angel a puzzled look. "You're all tensed up." She reached up to touch his shoulders, and Angel checked behind himself again. *This is really starting to get annoying,* she thought. Tia folded her arms across her chest and stared at Angel.

"I'm sorry, Tee," Angel said finally, leaning down and talking in a low voice. "I guess I'm just kind of nervous. I don't want to screw anything up."

Tia suddenly felt bad for having been so short with Angel. It *was* his first night on the job. She leaned in to give him a supportive kiss.

"Hey! Desmond! Quit flirting with the customers and get to those tables!" a booming voice called out. Tia lost her balance and nearly fell over.

She grasped the bar and looked up to see a short man, about five-three, with a large gut and thinning black hair, ambling toward Angel. *This must be the boss man,* she thought, studying him. Despite his small stature, Tia noticed that he had an intimidating presence. Aside from the voice that sounded like it could command armies, he had small, dark eyes—so dark, they were almost black—and the lines on his brow suggested that he spent most of his time scowling. Tia instantly disliked him.

Angel's posture had become rigid again. "I'm on my way, Mr. Walker," he said obediently. He was standing tall, but his eyes betrayed his nervousness.

Tia glared at Mr. Walker. *I don't dislike that little man,* she thought. *I hate him.*

"Yeah, I can see that," the short man said sarcastically, eyeing Tia. Something about his stare made Tia want to slap him. She looked at Andy and knew instantly that he was as unimpressed with Angel's boss as she was. His jaw might as well have been on the bar.

"Look, Desmond," Mr. Walker said, his voice sounding like a bad imitation of a New York gangster's, "it's a Saturday night—busiest night of the week—and I can't afford to have my employees slacking off." He looked at Andy briefly before his eyes fell on Tia again. "No matter how cute the customers may be," he said, winking at her. Tia suddenly wished she had a towel to wrap around herself—she felt like she was in one of those dreams where she showed up for school totally naked.

She saw Angel's jaw clench and his hands ball into fists, but he said nothing. Tia's heart fell. If any other guy had looked at her that way, she and Andy would have had to tackle Angel to hold him back.

"Now, get to work," Mr. Walker finished. He raked his gaze over Tia one last time before turning and walking to the end of the bar.

Tia stared up at Angel in disbelief, wondering how much of this he'd already put up with tonight.

"I can't believe you let him talk to you that way!"

Angel shrugged and smiled weakly. "He's just tense because we're understaffed," he said.

"I don't care if he's on the verge of a heart attack because all the grease from his oily little scalp has leaked into his arteries," she said. "No one treats you that way!" Angel put his hand on Tia's and looked into her eyes.

"It's only the first night, baby," he said. "It'll get better." Tia stared at him in disbelief. Was that all he could say? "I gotta go clear some tables," he continued. "You two all set for now?"

"I'm good," Andy said, holding up one hand.

Tia kept staring at Angel, waiting for him to get angry, yell back at his boss, quit, storm out of there—anything. But the longer she looked, the clearer it became that none of that was going to happen.

"I'm fine," she said finally, unable to manage anything else.

Angel squeezed her hand. "I'll be back soon," he said. Tia watched him leave and then turned to face Andy.

"*What* was *that?*" she demanded, as if Andy had an answer for her. "I can't believe this," she went on, running one hand through her long, dark hair. "This is even worse than I thought it was going to be."

Andy leaned closer to Tia. "Hey, don't get too

upset," he told her. "Like Angel said, it's only the first night. It's gotta get better."

Tia glared at Mr. Walker, who was flirting with some blonde at the end of the bar. "I don't know, Andy," she said. "I have a feeling this is as good as it gets."

# Angel Desmond

<u>What Mr. Walker told me to do:</u>

-Be on time.

-Take good care of the people in your section.

-Put all of your tips in the pool.

<u>What he really meant:</u>

-If you say more than three words to any one customer, you're flirting. Stop it.

-If you smile too much, you're goofing off. Get back to work.

-If your friends come in, you're obviously giving out free drinks—cut it out.

-If you look happy, you must be

pocketing extra tip money—put it in the pool!

—If you're two seconds late, I'll hassle you.

—If you leave a minute early, I'll fire you.

—If your section gets dirty, I'll dock your pay.

And finally . . .

—If you work hard and treat everyone with respect, you must be hiding something, and when I figure out what it is, I'll get you for it.

# CHAPTER
## *Getting into Character*
**3**

Jessica glanced at the clock as she walked into House of Java. *Six A.M.*, she thought, allowing herself a huge yawn. *I can't believe I'm awake.* She and Elizabeth had stayed up talking until midnight, and then Jessica had written in her new journal for an hour or so. At least she worked in a coffee place. A couple of cappuccinos and she'd be ready to go.

Jessica trudged into the back room to drop off her bag and fill in her time card. As she turned the corner, she was greeted by a welcome sight. Jeremy was standing in the center of the room, tying the strings of his apron around his waist.

"Good morning?" he said, looking at her tentatively.

"It is now," Jessica responded, feeling a smile creep onto her tired face.

Jeremy smiled easily at Jessica, warming her heart. He always looked at her with an unmasked admiration in his eyes that made Jessica feel truly special. He walked up to her and slipped his arms around her, clasping his hands behind her back. Jessica's heart skipped a few beats as he brought his lips to hers and kissed her softly. He smelled like peppermint. When he pulled back, Jessica stared giddily into his eyes.

"I gotta tell you, Jess," he said, grinning. "You look like hell."

Jessica scowled. "Gee, thanks," she said sarcastically, pushing him away. "And that charm school you went to really paid off." Jeremy chuckled as Jessica plucked her time card from the rack on the wall.

"Actually," she continued, pressing the card against the wall as she wrote in her arrival time, "Liz and I were up pretty late last night. You know—the whole Conner thing."

"She hasn't snapped out of it yet, huh?" Jeremy asked as Jessica replaced her card.

"Nope," Jessica said with a sigh. "She's really not doing too well."

"I thought you might need some cheering up." Jeremy's mouth curved into a mischievous grin. "So I brought you something."

Suddenly Jessica remembered the journal. "I know," she said, straightening up and smiling at him. "That was so sweet of you."

Jeremy narrowed his eyes. "What do you mean?" he asked. "I haven't even given it to you yet."

Jessica looked at Jeremy's confused expression. *What's he talking about?* she thought. *Didn't he leave me the journal yesterday?*

"You haven't given it to me yet," Jessica finally

managed. It was a baffled statement, not a question.

"Nooo . . . ," Jeremy said. He gestured at the table behind him. There were two place settings arranged, each with a steaming cup of coffee and a fresh muffin. In the center of the table was a single red rose, standing in an old, green soda bottle.

"I know how you hate the early morning shifts," Jeremy said, "so I got here early and started the brewing."

Jessica's heart warmed, her confusion forgotten. She smiled and looked up at Jeremy. "Only you would know that the way to a girl's heart is through her caffeine addiction."

"Oh, so now I'm abetting an addict, huh?" Jeremy said, turning to the table. "Maybe I should just throw the coffee out."

"No!" Jessica cried, grabbing his arm. "Don't make me hurt you, Aames."

Laughing, Jeremy hugged her again, his brown eyes twinkling. "You can hurt me anytime, baby," he said in a ridiculously deep voice.

"Ugh! Get away!" Jessica said, pushing him back. She plopped down on the couch and grabbed a muffin, picking off a little chunk from the top.

"You know," she said, popping her muffin bit into her mouth as Jeremy sat down next to her, "I think I'm going to write about this in my new journal." She expected Jeremy to crack a smile or give some kind of indication that he knew he'd been busted. Nothing.

"I didn't know you kept a journal," Jeremy said.

Jessica's brow furrowed as she watched him peel the wrapper from his muffin. *Either he's the best liar I've ever met, or he really didn't leave me that gift.*

Tia picked up the phone and punched in the seven-digit number that had become so automatic, she didn't even have to watch her fingers anymore. And when Angel's sleepy voice answered, she smiled as she always did when she heard him for the first time each day.

"I love it when I'm the first one you talk to in the morning," she said in a breathy voice.

Angel chuckled. "Yeah? Is that why you're always waking me up on Sunday mornings?" he asked.

"You got it," Tia answered quickly. "That and the fact that my brothers are about as quiet as a herd of buffalo. I've been up since seven-thirty. What time is it now?" She could hear Angel fumbling around, searching for something, and she knew he must still be in bed. She imagined him under the covers, wearing nothing but baggy boxers, and felt her face start to heat up. Suddenly she heard a small crash and knew he'd uncovered the alarm clock on his bedside table. Most of the time it was covered with car magazines, newspapers, and whatever book Angel was reading at the time.

"Eight-thirty," he answered groggily.

"Ooh, sorry," Tia said, grimacing. "I should have let you sleep in a little longer."

"Nah, I should be getting up anyway," he said, his voice still raspy with sleep. "I've got to get ready for work."

Tia laughed. "Honey, I think you're hallucinating," she said. "You worked last night. This is Sunday morning. You don't have to work today." Angel hesitated just long enough to make Tia uneasy. "Do you?" she asked tentatively.

"Uh, actually." Angel paused to clear his throat. "Yeah, I do. Mr. Walker asked me to take the brunch shift today."

"Brunch?" Tia asked, coiling the phone cord around her finger. "Since when does the Riot do brunch?"

"This is the first day," Angel answered through a yawn. "Mr. Walker's trying it out for a while to see how it goes, so I have to be in at ten to start the prep work."

"Oh," Tia said flatly, letting the phone cord drop. "I guess that means breakfast is out of the question."

"Yeah, sorry, baby," Angel said. Tia could tell from the sound of his voice that he really did feel bad about it. *I will not get upset,* she told herself. *If he has to work, he has to work. I'm not going to be one of those girlfriends who makes him feel guilty every time he has something else to do.*

"That's okay," Tia said, trying to sound upbeat. "Maybe we can do dinner instead," she offered. Angel hesitated again, and Tia's heart dropped.

"Well," he started slowly, "I was thinking of asking Mr. Walker if I could stay through the night shift too. He's really short staffed, so I know he needs help, and I could definitely use the money."

"Isn't that a really long time to work?" Tia asked, aware that she was beginning to sound annoyed. "I mean, this is only your first weekend. You don't want to burn yourself out," she added, hoping to sound more reasonable. While she was waiting for Angel's reply, her youngest brother, Tomás, who was six, came running down the hall.

"Tia!" he cried, his black bangs hanging down over his forehead. "Jesse and Miguel won't let me play, and it's my turn!" When he was close enough, Tia scooped him up and balanced him on her hip.

"*Uno momento*, Tomás," she said. "I'm talking to Angel." Tomás's little face lit up, and he leaned toward the receiver.

"Hi, Angel!" he yelled, an irresistible grin on his face. Tia heard Angel laughing on the other end of the phone, and she had to laugh herself.

"Okay, Tomás," she said, setting him down and squatting so that she was at his level. "You go back in the living room. I'll be right in, and we'll *make* Jesse and Miguel give you a turn, *está bien?*" Tomás nodded and ran back down the hall.

"He loves you, you know," Tia said, resuming her conversation with Angel.

"I think he's pretty cool too," Angel answered. "Make sure you tell him I said hi back."

"I will," Tia said, smiling. She enjoyed the way Angel had become a part of her family. Both of her parents loved him, and all her brothers did too. Especially Tomás. As far as he was concerned, Angel was another one of his brothers. After all, he'd been around for as long as Tomás could remember.

"So anyway," Tia said, "we were talking about your work schedule, right?" She heard Angel exhale loudly and had a feeling there was something he hadn't told her yet. "It's not always going to be this hectic, is it?" she asked, doing her best to be understanding. "I mean, you didn't sign on for slave labor. He has to give you a break, right?" She had hoped Angel would think she was being funny, but he wasn't laughing.

Instead he took another deep breath. Tia braced herself—she was definitely about to be hit with something. "I wanted to talk to you about this in person," he said, "but I guess I might as well tell you now."

"Tell me what?" Tia said, not sure if she really wanted to hear the answer.

"Well," Angel said, his voice heavy, "last night when I got home, I talked to my father, and he said he's going to have to cut back my hours at the garage."

"I'm sorry, baby," Tia said automatically.

"Yeah, it kind of sucks," Angel said. "And I have to make up the money somewhere. . . ."

"So you're going to work more hours at the Riot," Tia said. Frustrated tears welled up in her eyes, but she blinked them back.

"Yeah. Are you upset?"

"No," Tia lied, wondering how she and Angel were ever going to have any time together if she was in school all day and he was working afternoons and evenings. "You've got to do what you've got to do, right?"

"I guess so," Angel responded, sounding broken. "I'm really sorry, Tee."

Tia forced herself to remain calm. If it wasn't so clear that Angel was as upset about his job situation as she was, she might have been mad. But hearing the desperation in his voice, Tia knew she couldn't make him feel any worse about it.

"Don't be sorry," she said. "It won't be that bad. I mean, last night was kind of stressful, but it *was* your first night. After a while Mr. Walker will lay off and you'll get into a routine, and we'll find a way to spend more time together."

"Ya think?" Angel said, actually starting to sound hopeful.

*No,* Tia thought. "Absolutely," she replied. "Besides, if nothing else, your freak of a boss will provide you with lots of great story material."

Angel actually chuckled. "Tee, have I told you how amazing you are?" he asked. Tia could see the smile in his eyes, even over the phone.

"Not today," she said coyly.

"Well, you are. You're the absolute best," Angel said. "Thanks for understanding."

"No problem," Tia said, twisting one strand of her hair around her index finger. "I'm sure everything will work out fine." It was a lie, but at least it seemed to make Angel feel better.

*He's doing this for me,* Tia reminded herself. *So he'll have enough money to come visit on weekends when he starts college.* The least she could do in return was try to make it a little easier for him.

"So then when I got out of work, I found this note tucked under the windshield of the Jeep," Jessica explained, her eyes wide.

"Are you sure it's for you?" Tia asked with a teasing smile. "I mean, were there little notes stuck on everyone's windshield or just yours?" Maria stifled a laugh as Jessica narrowed her eyes at Tia.

"Of course I'm sure it's for me," she snapped. "My *name* is on it," she said, pulling an envelope from her bag and waving it in front of Tia. Maria had to laugh. These two were turning mutual antagonism into an art form.

"All right, all right," Tia said, holding up her hands. "Don't bite my head off. I was just making sure." She grabbed a handful of popcorn from the circular, glass table on Maria's patio and sat back in her lounge chair.

"Well?" Maria jumped in. "What does it say?" Jessica pulled a piece of paper from the envelope. She unfolded it with a flourish, cleared her throat, and read it aloud dramatically.

*"Of all sad words of tongue or pen,*
*The saddest are these: 'It might have been!'"*

Jessica refolded the paper and looked up at her friends.

"Hey," Tia said, "that's John Greenleaf Whittier, isn't it?"

Jessica's jaw dropped. She looked down at the paper and then back at Tia. "How did you know that?" she demanded.

Tia scowled. "Don't look so surprised. I happen to enjoy reading a little poetry in my spare time," she said, looking down her nose at Jessica. "Besides, if you'd been paying attention in English class the other day, you'd recognize it too. Mrs. O'Reilly wrote it on the board."

"Oh," Jessica said, her voice flat. She picked up her bottled water and took a long sip.

Maria chuckled. "Can I see it?" she said. She plucked the paper from Jessica's outstretched hand and scanned it quickly. "I doubt Jeremy's the one who left you this poem. It sounds more like the kind of thing you'd get from someone who *wishes* he was dating you—or maybe even someone you used to date."

"The question is, *who?*" Jessica said, looking back and forth between Tia and Maria.

Tia shrugged and threw a piece of popcorn into the air, catching it in her mouth. "Whoever it is can't know you too well," she said.

"Why's that?" Jessica asked, frowning her brow.

"Well, he gave you the journal and then this poem," Tia said. "He seems to be under the impression that you can read and write." Tia giggled and shielded herself with her hands as Jessica threw a fistful of popcorn at her.

"Look," Maria said, ignoring their antics and leaning forward, "could it be someone in your English class?"

Jessica bit her lip and looked at Tia. "Can you think of anyone?"

Tia paused for a moment and then shook her head. "Not really. I mean, it could be anybody. You're pretty dateable."

Maria laughed, but Jessica looked offended. "*Dateable?*" she repeated. "Oh, gee, Tia, thanks for the compliment."

Now Tia was laughing too. "I meant it in a nice way," she assured Jessica between giggles.

Jessica rolled her eyes. "Well, thank you, but even

if you did, it's not true. Don't forget—I'm still a social leper around here. Whoever it is has to be pretty brave to go after the outcast."

Maria half-smiled. She couldn't get used to Jessica Wakefield talking about herself in less than glowing terms. Somehow it did make her a lot easier to hang out with.

"So is there anyone brave enough in your English class?" Maria asked. "If the poem was on the board the other day, it kind of makes sense that he might use it to give you a clue."

"Ugh! I'm sorry, but this whole thing is so dorky!" Tia exclaimed.

"What do you mean?" Jessica asked defensively, eyeing the note.

"Number one, if the guy likes you, why doesn't he just tell you?"

"Because—"

Tia raised her hand. "I wasn't finished."

Jessica snapped her mouth shut and scowled.

"And number two," Tia continued. "If he *is* going to do the whole secret-admirer thing, why doesn't he write his *own* poem? It's such a cop-out."

"Well, I think it's romantic," Maria said.

"Exactly!" Jessica agreed. "And not everyone's a poet, Tee. Maybe he can't express himself. Or maybe he's just . . . I don't know . . . *shy*."

"Wait a minute," Tia said, sitting up straight. "What about Will?"

All the color drained from Jessica's face as if someone had popped a hole in her and squeezed it out. "No. Not possible."

"Why not?" Tia said, still munching. "He just broke up with Melissa, right?"

"Nuh-uh," Jessica said. "First of all, he said he just wants to be friends, and second, he can't have gotten over being Melissa-whipped that fast. He doesn't have the guts."

"But—"

"No. It's not him," Jessica said firmly. "Let's move on."

"Fine," Tia said moodily, leaning back again. "Shoot me down."

"Okay. Back to English class," Maria said nervously. Jessica seemed pretty shaken.

"I don't know," Tia said, looking at Jessica. "I mean, it's basically just Will, Andy—whose idea of poetry is a good dirty limerick—and a bunch of other jocks. Not exactly prime candidates for a *love connection.*"

"I'm sure Mrs. O'Reilly has more than one section of senior English," Maria offered, helping herself to a carrot stick.

"That's true," Jessica agreed, regaining her composure a bit. "I just can't believe I have a secret admirer. I finally find the perfect guy, and now Mr. Random wants to romance me."

"Are you going to tell Jeremy?" Tia asked.

"No way," Jessica said without hesitation.

"Why not?" Maria asked. "Don't you think he'd want to know?"

"Look, I thought about this on the way over here," Jessica said. "First of all, Jeremy and I just started going out. If I tell him, he might get all paranoid and threatened for no reason. And trust me when I tell you that boy *does not* need one more thing to worry about."

"Are you sure?" Tia asked, twisting her hair into a sloppy bun. "Secrets are not a good thing."

"It's not a real secret," Jessica said sternly. "This is nothing. And it's not like I'm going to *do* anything with this guy. So I would be stressing Jeremy out for no reason."

Tia shrugged and picked up her script. "It's your call. But I reserve the right to say 'I told you so' when the time comes."

"Fine," Jessica said, grabbing her script. "Let's get back to work. I only have an hour. If I'm late for dinner, Mrs. Pervis will yell at me in that fake British accent of hers."

Maria laughed. "Let's cram, then. I need all the practice I can get if I'm gonna have this part down by Saturday night."

"Please," Tia said, standing and curling one leg underneath herself as she sat back down. "Jessica, will you tell Julia Roberts over there she's probably going to get an Oscar for this role—or an Emmy or a Tony—whatever they give out for plays?"

"I think you're exaggerating a little," Maria said modestly.

"No, she's not," Jessica said. "You're obviously a natural actor, Maria. It even shows in drama class. Why else would Ms. Delaney have offered you the part?"

Maria was really flattered by their comments, but clearly they were overstating things. "Thanks, guys," she said. "But I'm still going to need all the practice I can get between now and next weekend."

"Well, then, let's get going," Tia said, thumbing through her script. "Where did we stop anyway?"

Maria was about to answer when the glass door slid open. She and her friends looked up, and none of them managed to mask their surprise.

"Hey, Ken," Maria said.

Ken stood frozen with one hand on the door handle and glanced at Tia and Jessica. "Your mom didn't say you had company," he said.

"Ken Matthews," Tia said, grinning up at him. "I don't think we've been formally introduced, but aren't you in my *English* class?" Tia shot a sideways glance at Jessica, who rolled her eyes.

"Yeah, I guess," Ken said, shoving his hands into the front pockets of his wrinkled khaki shorts.

Maria looked from Jessica to Ken and back again. *Could it be?* she wondered. *They did date once.* Maria felt an inexplicable nervous flutter in her stomach, but it only lasted a moment. There was no way. Ken

61

and Jessica had ended pretty badly, and she had a feeling Ken wouldn't want to go there again. Too much baggage.

"Ken, this is Tia Ramirez," Maria said. "Don't mind her. She's a bit . . . weird." Tia scowled at Maria and started flipping through her script again.

"Hey," Ken said.

"So what brings you here?" Maria asked. Ken shuffled his feet and looked down at the ground for a moment.

"I just wanted to find out how your rehearsal went," he mumbled. He looked up at her, and Maria couldn't help noticing how the blue in his T-shirt made his eyes stand out against his lightly tanned skin. "And, you know . . . see if there was anything I could do to help you out."

"Actually, there is," Maria said. "You could sit down and read with us."

Tia and Jessica both shifted in their seats, but Maria refused to look at them. She didn't want Ken to pick up on a bunch of surprised glances. She wanted him to feel welcome.

"Okay," Ken said slowly.

"Great!" Maria said. "We were just about to start the last scene, and it would really help if you could read the male lead." Ken nodded, but his feet seemed to be firmly rooted to the ground.

"You can look on with me," Jessica offered, to Maria's surprise.

"All right," Ken said. He glanced quickly at Maria, then walked around the table to sit next to Jessica.

"I'm gonna grab another water from the cooler," Tia said, standing up. "Do you want anything, Ken?"

Maria grinned. Of course Tia and Jessica were going to try to make Ken comfortable. Could she have expected any less from two people who practically had *sociable* stamped across their foreheads?

Tia tossed Ken a soda, and he actually smiled. Maria was amazed. She couldn't believe that Ken, who was barely speaking to *anyone* just a few weeks ago, was now willing read aloud with them just to help her rehearse for a play. For that matter, it was pretty incredible that Tia and Jessica had been so quick to offer to help her out too.

*I guess doing this play was a pretty good decision,* Maria told herself, believing for the first time that she might actually be ready opening night. And she realized as she looked around at her guests that she hadn't even thought about Conner all day. *Maybe I'm finally getting over him. Maybe my luck is finally beginning to change.*

# Will Simmons

Today was Melissa's first day back at school. She was coming into homeroom with a late pass just as I was on my way out. I tried to make eye contact with her, but she wouldn't even look in my direction. I guess that's the way it's gonna be for a while. I just hope we can be friends again someday. I sound like a skipping CD. I said the same thing to Jess the other night. She said it was possible, but for all I know she just said that so I'd leave her alone. After all, she has a boyfriend now. She doesn't need me hanging around.

But that's probably just as well. It wouldn't be good for Melissa to see me talking to Jessica all over the place anyway. I'm not sure she could handle it.

So I'm just going to have to steer clear of Jessica—for now.

# melissa Fox

Cherie—
Every time I walk into a class, everybody stops talking and just stares. It's like they all think I'm some kind of freak or something.

You guys could have told me I was the major topic of conversation around here <u>before</u> I came back to school, you know.

          —melissa


P.S. I don't think I can handle House of java this afternoon. maybe tomorrow. Or Wednesday. Or next week. Or never.

# CHAPTER 4
# A Kiss Is Still a Kiss

"So tell me," Jessica said in the husky voice of her character, Sadie the waitress, "did you come here for the chocolate cake, or were you planning to kiss me?" Charlie Rucker moved closer to her, so close that their faces were only an inch apart. He stared at her with steely blue eyes that were so intense, Jessica almost forgot he was acting.

"Why tell you when I can show you?" he said, grabbing her shoulders forcefully and pulling her to him. Jessica gasped, but she tried to stay in character. Charlie kissed her passionately, and he seemed to know what he was doing, so she tried to return the kiss with equal fervor. She didn't want to look like a prude who couldn't handle the steamy character she was supposed to be playing. Charlie moved his hands up her back and into her hair. Jessica felt a shiver down her spine, and without thinking, she wrapped her arms tightly around his neck. Then with a gentle push at her shoulders, Charlie pulled himself away and left Jessica standing there with her lips throbbing.

It was then that Jessica realized that other members of the cast had started to whistle and cheer. She could even hear Tia and Maria catcalling from backstage. But Charlie wasn't fazed. He looked Jessica squarely in the eye and delivered his line flawlessly.

"Does that answer your question?" he said. Jessica nodded weakly. It was all she could manage, and thankfully, it was all her character was supposed to do.

"Cut! Perfect! Let's take five, everyone!" called Ms. Delaney, approaching the stage. "Great job, Jessica," she said enthusiastically. Jessica was glad to hear the praise since she could hardly remember a single moment of the scene she'd just performed.

"You know," Ms. Delaney continued with a twinkle in her eye, "if it weren't for the look on your face, I'd think you and Charlie had been rehearsing that kiss for weeks."

The cast members around them started laughing, and Jessica felt a four-alarm blush take over her face. She glanced over at Charlie, but to her surprise, he had already disappeared into the wings. Jessica's blush deepened. She was standing center stage—hot, flushed, and mortified. And Charlie hadn't even had the courtesy to stick around and be embarrassed with her.

"Talk about hot and heavy," Maria said, whistling as she and Tia approached Jessica.

"Are you sure you and Charlie haven't been rehearsing in secret, Jess?" Tia teased, jabbing Jessica with her elbow.

"Oh, yeah, right." Jessica took a step back and scowled. "Like I'd cheat on Jeremy with Charlie Rucker!"

Maria laughed. Charlie was a little on the serious side, but he was smart and cute and he sure knew how to dress. He didn't seem like such a bad choice to Maria.

"Who said anything about cheating?" Tia said with mock innocence. "I wouldn't accuse you of something like that. I'm just saying that kiss was a little over the top."

"More like over the top and down the other side," Maria added, unable to resist.

Jessica exhaled sharply. "Oh, come on, you guys," she pleaded. "It wasn't me. It was Charlie. He was all over me."

"Mm-hmm," Tia responded, nodding. "And I suppose he made you wrap your arms around him too?"

Jessica's face reddened slightly, but she didn't look away. "At least I didn't flub my lines so badly that the director had to take five," she shot back.

"She's got you there, Tia," Maria said between giggles.

"It wasn't that bad," Tia asserted, placing her hands on her hips, but that only made Maria laugh more.

"Not at all," Jessica said sarcastically. "Lots of people pronounce the word *subpoenas* like it's a part of the male anatomy."

Tia picked up one of the white ceramic dishes from a table on the set and held it in front of her face to hide her embarrassed blush. "All right," she conceded. "I guess that was pretty bad." She composed herself and replaced the plate. Then with an exaggerated look of longing, she pressed both hands over her heart and added, "I guess I was just thinking of . . . Charlie."

"You are so sick," Jessica said as Maria and Tia dissolved into hysterical giggles. She walked past the bar stools and the pale green Formica counter and around the mock cash register toward the edge of the stage. Maria followed, trying to control her laughter, and sat down heavily, allowing her legs to dangle over the side. Jessica and Tia did the same.

Maria noticed that the muscles in her face actually felt a little sore and rubbed her cheekbones. It had been a while since she'd laughed that hard. She glanced at Tia and Jessica out of the corner of her eye, hardly able to believe that she was hanging out with them and enjoying herself. For a while she'd been jealous of Tia's relationship with Elizabeth, and she and Jessica had never gotten along until recently. It was amazing how quickly things could change.

"Oh—Tia," Jessica began, sitting up straight and leaning forward to look at her friend. "I've been meaning to ask you, was Angel's second night of work any better than the first?"

Tia rolled her eyes and sighed, leaning back heavily on her elbows. "I wouldn't know," she said, staring out at the auditorium seats. "I called his house at ten last night, and he still wasn't home. I haven't talked to him in, like, forever."

"That's too bad," Maria said. It was obvious that Angel's work situation was already getting to Tia.

"How about Liz? Is she doing any better?" Tia asked Jessica. Maria stiffened a little at the question and looked away, trying to appear disinterested. Part of her was glad Tia had asked, but at the same time she felt like she was eavesdropping on a conversation she had no business hearing.

Jessica shrugged. "Not really. She's been a mess ever since Conner threw her out. She didn't leave her room all weekend, and I don't think she talked to anyone at school today. I mean, she'll cry to me about it at night, but during the day it's like she's completely closed off."

Maria stared at her feet and knocked her heels against the stage until she realized that the conversation had stopped. When she turned her head, she found that both Jessica and Tia were staring at her.

"You should really talk to Liz," Jessica said.

Maria trained her eyes on the ceiling. "I'm not sure that's such a good idea," she answered, shaking her head almost imperceptibly.

"Look," Tia said, her voice gentle but imposing. "I know this hasn't been easy for you, but Liz is really down. And you two are best friends. Are you seriously going to let a *guy* come between you?"

"I'm not the one who let him come between us," Maria said quietly. *So why do I feel guilty?* she thought.

Jessica pulled up her legs and wrapped her arms around her knees. "Liz feels terrible for lying to you about Conner," she said. "If she could, she'd undo this whole mess."

"So would I," Maria said, her voice barely above a whisper.

"So talk to her," Tia suggested, hanging her arm loosely around Maria's shoulders. "You'll feel a lot better if you get it all out in the open."

"You really think so?" Maria asked, squinting skeptically.

"Absolutely," Jessica responded. Then she half-smiled. "Besides, I can't take the girl anymore. I'll pay you to take her off my hands."

Maria looked up at the muted stage lights and sighed. How was she supposed to talk to Elizabeth when the mere thought of it made her heart leap into her throat?

"If you can get up here and act in front of a bunch of strangers, you can get up the guts to talk to your best friend for five minutes," Tia said.

Maria smirked. Tia sure had a way of cutting

through the bull. "All right," she said finally. "I'll give it a try." Jessica's face lit up, and Tia squeezed her shoulder, but Maria was just hoping she wouldn't regret her words.

The idea of hashing it out with Elizabeth gave her more stage fright than being in the spotlight ever could.

"All right, people, that's it for today," Ms. Delaney called. "But remember, tomorrow *everyone* needs to be off script. If you're having trouble with your lines, I suggest you chat with Ms. Slater, who appears to have memorized her entire part in just two days." Tia, Jessica, and several other members of the cast applauded, and Ms. Delaney paused to look at Maria, who was staring down at her clasped hands modestly.

"See? Everyone loves you," Jessica whispered, elbowing Maria, but Maria just shrugged it off.

"I'll see you all back here tomorrow afternoon at three-thirty. Good job today, everybody," Ms. Delaney finished, clapping as she did at the end of every rehearsal.

"Congratulations, Maria," Tia said as all three girls turned and headed for the dressing room. "I still can't believe you have the whole play memorized."

"I know," Jessica chimed in. "It feels like you've been rehearsing with us the whole time."

"Thanks," Maria said, pushing open the dressing-room door and holding it for Tia and Jessica. "I'm glad I haven't thrown anybody off by coming into it so late."

"Are you kidding?" Tia asked as she passed through the door. "If anything, you've improved the play just by being in it."

"And Ms. Delaney is obviously impressed too," Jessica added, following Tia. "I think she's ready to cast you in the spring play right now." Jessica had only taken a few steps into the dressing room when Tia stopped suddenly, causing Jessica to bump into her.

"What are you doing?" Jessica asked when she had regained her footing.

"Um, Jess," Tia started. "Is that your bag?" she asked, pointing to a large black duffel bag under the makeup table. Jessica followed Tia's gaze to see two balloons floating in front of the dressing-room mirror. She stared for a moment, confused, before looking down to see what was anchoring them. There, on top of her bag, was a small, black, velvet box.

"The secret admirer strikes again," Maria said dramatically. Jessica walked past Tia and over to her bag. She picked up the box and sat down on one of the padded stools to examine it. When she opened it, she couldn't believe her eyes. Inside was a gorgeous silver necklace. Its delicate herringbone pattern sparkled, reflecting the lights around the mirror.

"This is beautiful," Jessica said, lifting it out of the box and draping it around her neck. She watched her friends' reflections in the mirror and then turned around to let them see the necklace.

Tia took it from Jessica's hand and held it up to the light. "It's not cheap either. See the numbers 925 there?" she said, holding it out so Jessica could see the clasp. Jessica nodded. "When we went down to one of the markets in Tijuana once, my grandmother told me that's how you tell the good silver from the inexpensive stuff. Look for the 925."

Jessica slowly took the necklace back from Tia and ran it across her hand. It felt smooth and cold against her skin. "There's no way Jeremy could afford this," she said, her heart falling. Up until now she'd held out the hope that Jeremy was the romantic guy leaving her random tokens of his affection. Now she was just confused.

"Hey! There's a card," Maria said. She snatched one of the balloons from the air, detached an envelope, and handed it to Jessica.

Jessica tore open the envelope and looked at the card. "It's not signed," she said, disappointed. "Just another poem."

"Well . . . ," Tia prodded. "What does it say?"

Jessica cleared her throat and read out loud.

*"You must remember this, a kiss is still a kiss,*
*A sigh is just a sigh."*

"I love that song," Tia exclaimed when Jessica had finished reading.

Jessica turned to Tia. "You know it?" she asked, surprised.

"Oh, come on, Jess. Where have you been? It's from *Casablanca*," Tia answered matter-of-factly. "Angel and I have seen it like ten times. You know— Bogart, Bergman, love, war."

"Oh, right." Jessica nodded. "That's one of Liz's favorite movies. She and her boring ex must've watched it every other week for a year."

"Can I see that?" Maria asked, gesturing at the card. When Jessica passed it to her, she studied it for a moment before looking up.

"I think this is a clue," she said finally.

"What do you mean?" Jessica said, practically jumping off her stool in excitement.

"Well," Maria said slowly. "Think about it. The quote is about a *kiss*. The importance of a *kiss*. What does that make you think of?" She lowered her chin and looked up at Jessica through her lashes.

"Um . . . kissing?" Jessica said, clueless.

"No!" Tia cried, grinning in triumph. "Charlie Rucker!"

"No!" Jessica gasped, her eyes widening.

"Yes!" Maria said. "Who else could it be? You rehearsed your kiss today, and you said yourself that he was really into it."

Suddenly Jessica felt short of breath. "Oh my

76

God," she said, covering her mouth with one hand. "You're right. I got the journal on Saturday after play practice, and—"

"—and Charlie left rehearsal early that day for a family dinner or something," Maria finished, pointing with her index finger. "I remember because that was my first day, and we had to cut short our last scene together so he could go."

"But what about the note?" Jessica asked. "How would he know when I'd be at work?"

Tia lowered one eyebrow. "Please," she scoffed. "Charlie sucks down coffee by the gallon. He's, like, *always* at House of Java. He was probably there Sunday morning—you just didn't notice."

Jessica's heart was pounding in her ears. "I hope I haven't been sending him signals or anything while we've been rehearsing." She turned to Tia and Maria. "You don't think he thinks I like him just because our characters are supposed to have something going on, do you?"

"He might," Maria answered. "A lot of actors get into relationships because they confuse stage romance with real romance."

Jessica groaned and pressed her hand to her forehead.

"Then again," Maria continued, "he is sending you these things anonymously. That's usually a sign that the admirer isn't sure if you like him or not."

"That's true," Tia answered. "But guys don't do this kind of stuff just because some chick makes them sweat. He's got a serious thing for you."

Jessica put her elbows on the makeup table and propped her head in her hands, staring at her friends in the mirror. "I can't keep all this stuff," she said, sighing. "I mean, Charlie's cute, and he's probably a nice guy, but I have a boyfriend."

Tia put the back of her hand to her forehead dramatically. "Help, my life is so hard," she mimicked in a high voice. "I have a perfect boyfriend and a really cute guy leaving me expensive gifts. What am I going to do?"

Maria laughed, but Jessica narrowed her eyes and glared at Tia. "Very funny," Jessica sneered. "It may sound stupid, but it is a problem." She placed the necklace back in the box and closed it, holding it firmly in her hand.

"So what are you going to do?" Maria asked, folding her arms across her chest.

Jessica turned around on the makeup stool. "The only thing I can do," she said plainly. "I'm going to find Charlie in school tomorrow and return the gifts."

"You're kidding!" Tia screeched, staring at the box in Jessica's hand. "That necklace is gorgeous."

"Yeah, Jess," Maria said. "Six months ago you would've already had that thing around your neck."

Jessica looked Maria directly in the eye. "People change," she said, placing the box on top of her bag. "And right now, I'm a one-guy type of girl."

# Jeremy Aames

Halfway through my first date with Jennifer Klein, her laugh started to grate on me like fingernails on a chalkboard. It was so bad, I didn't kiss her good night, even though I knew she wanted me to.

Katie van Pelton said "like" so many times, I started counting. I got to 103 before she got mad and said I was "like, totally not listening."

I regretted dating Alexis Greene in less than ten minutes. We went to dinner, but she wouldn't eat. She ordered and everything, but when the food came, she claimed she wasn't hungry. Do girls really think that's attractive?

Then I started worrying that I was too critical or something. Like maybe I was destined to never have a girlfriend because I couldn't get past these little annoyances. But then I met Jessica.

And every time I uncover one of her "quirks," it just makes me like her more.

I love the way she crinkles her nose when she's thinking.

And how she always puts her hands on her hips when she's really serious about something.

And the fact that she's always drawing little hearts on everything.

And how she can't walk by a reflective surface without checking herself out—windows, mirrors, metal canisters—everything.

I even like the way she gets whipped cream on her nose every time she sips a hot chocolate at work.

I'm beginning to think I might finally have found the girl I've been looking for. I just hope she hasn't started figuring out all my little quirks.

# CHAPTER 5

*Mending Fences*

"Hey, you!" Jessica called out as she walked into House of Java later that evening.

Jeremy looked up from the cappuccino machine and grinned. "Hey, you."

Jessica slid onto a stool at the counter and watched Jeremy as he finished making up the order. He looked even more handsome than usual. His skin was deeply tanned from hours on the football field, and his shoulders flexed beneath his heather gray T-shirt as he moved. It was all Jessica could do to keep from leaning across the counter and grabbing him.

He turned around and winked at her before setting the cappuccino mug in front of his customer. Jessica's heart was fluttering uncontrollably. Like Charlie Rucker or any secret admirer could stand a chance against Jeremy. No one else could make her this spontaneously giddy.

Jeremy walked over and leaned on the counter in front of her. Jessica slid forward on the stool and kissed him on the mouth, letting her lips linger against his for an extended moment. "Can you take a break?" she asked huskily.

Jeremy smiled, his eyes at half-mast. "I think I have to now."

He untied his apron and told Corey Scott he was taking ten. Corey, who was flipping through some heavy-metal 'zine at the other end of the counter, just grunted.

As Jeremy rounded the counter, Jessica took his hand and smiled. "Is it me, or is Corey's hair purple?" she whispered.

"Yeah, and she got a new nose ring," Jeremy answered, leading Jessica through the café and out the back door. "I think she's trying to impress a new guy."

They stepped out into the courtyard behind House of Java, and Jessica smiled as a light breeze lifted her hair off her neck. There was a hippy-chick guitar soloist strumming away on the stage at the rear of the cobbled patio. Couples and small groups were seated at the mismatched tables dotting the courtyard. Jeremy led her over to an empty table near the border fence and pulled her onto his lap.

The moment Jessica was seated, Jeremy cuddled her into his arms and caught her lips in a deep, probing kiss. Jessica didn't even have time to catch her breath. By the time he broke away, her mind was swimming and she was gasping for air.

"I have good news," Jeremy said, grinning.

Jessica ran the tip of her finger along the edge of

his T-shirt collar, gently grazing his skin. Jeremy closed his eyes and smiled. "What is it?" Jessica asked.

Jeremy grabbed her hand and held it. "Stop doing that, or I won't be able to form a sentence."

Giggling, Jessica adopted a complacent look. "What's your news?"

"One of my dad's old business buddies might have a job for him," Jeremy said, his eyes bright.

Jessica's heart jumped, and she hugged him tightly. "That's wonderful!" she said as he squeezed her back.

"It's not definite yet," Jeremy said quickly. "But this guy is starting up a small computer firm, and he wants my dad to work with him. So if the investors come through . . ." He paused and gazed hopefully into Jessica's eyes. "God, it would be so great. Everything could go back to normal."

"I'm so happy for you," Jessica said, leaning into him and resting her head against his shoulder.

Jeremy kissed the top of her head and rested his chin against her hair. "Would you believe my mom actually laughed today?" he said quietly. "It was so weird. I didn't realize how long it had been."

"And how's your dad?" Jessica asked.

"He's excited, but he keeps telling us not to get our hopes up," Jeremy said. "Suddenly he's, like, Realistic Man." He said the last part in a low, announcer's voice, as if he were talking about a superhero.

Jessica laughed. "Well, that's good. I hope it all works out for him."

"Me too," Jeremy said.

Jessica took a deep breath of the cool evening air and sighed happily as Jeremy shifted his arms to make her more comfortable. She'd never seen him so relaxed and genuinely happy. As she listened to the sound of his breathing and felt his chest rising and falling, she started to think about what Tia had said at Maria's house yesterday. Maybe she should be honest with Jeremy about this secret-admirer thing. Now that the stress seemed to be lifting—

"Hey," Jeremy said, running a hand over her hair and sending chills down her spine. "Everything started to change when we got together, you know?"

Jessica looked up at him and smirked. "Oh, come on," she said, hitting him playfully. "What am I now, your good-luck charm?"

Jeremy smiled. "Maybe," he said. "You got a problem with that?"

Jessica felt a warm rush wash over her and found herself drowning in his deep brown eyes. "No," she said weakly, just before he lowered his face to hers and kissed her slowly and sweetly.

*Okay, I wasn't going to tell him because he was stressed, but now that he's so happy . . . I don't want to mess with that,* Jessica thought as she started to lose herself in his kiss.

It didn't matter anyway. Tomorrow she would

return the necklace to Charlie and the whole thing would be history.

"Here goes," Maria whispered to herself.

She took a deep breath and slowly opened the door to the *Oracle* office. It was quiet inside, except for the buzz of machinery—four computers that were virtually always on, a photocopier, a scanner, a laser printer, and of course, the fluorescent lights. Normally their humming sounds were drowned out by the clicking of keyboards and the voices of students working frantically to get out the weekly paper, but at 7:30 A.M., Maria felt like she was entering an abandoned factory.

She stepped in as quietly as her chunky boot heels would allow and looked around the wide room. It didn't take her long to spot Elizabeth sitting at a computer against the back wall, her hands in her lap and her shoulders hunched forward as she stared at the monitor. Obviously she hadn't heard Maria come in. *She's probably totally consumed by whatever article she's working on,* Maria thought.

But as she walked closer, Maria noticed that the computer screen was blank. "Writer's block?" she asked when she was close enough to speak without raising her voice.

Elizabeth lifted her head and straightened her posture. "Maria?" she asked, slowly turning in her chair. Elizabeth's eyes were so wide that Maria almost smiled, but then she remembered why she had come.

"Hi," Maria said simply. "What are you working on?" she asked, nodding at the computer screen.

Elizabeth exhaled heavily and looked at the monitor. "I have no idea," she said. "I've been sitting here for half an hour, and I don't think I've had one complete thought." She looked back at Maria with tired eyes. "My mind's all over the place."

*Wow,* Maria thought, observing Elizabeth's dazed expression. Jessica had said Elizabeth was pretty out of it, but Maria had never seen her this unfocused before.

"I'm sorry about Conner," Maria said quietly. Elizabeth winced at the mention of his name. *I can relate to that,* Maria thought.

"Yeah." Elizabeth sighed wearily. "I guess I've messed things up all around." She gazed up at Maria, her eyes glassy, as if she were about to cry. "I'm so sorry, Maria. I should have been honest with you from the beginning, but I just kept thinking that my feelings for him would go away, or that you'd stop liking him, or . . . something." Elizabeth ran one hand through her blond hair. "I don't know," she finished, looking down.

"I do," Maria said, pulling out the chair next to Elizabeth and taking a seat. "And it's not all your fault."

Elizabeth stared up at Maria. "Of course it's my fault."

Maria shook her head. "Not completely," she said,

fully realizing her role in the whole fiasco for the first time. "I was acting like a total idiot over Conner. One minute I was telling everyone I was over him, and the next minute I was trying to get him alone and make him fall in love with me."

"Still, I should have told you how I felt about him," Elizabeth said. "I should have known that you weren't over him yet."

"And I should have been straight with you," Maria said, looking Elizabeth directly in the eye. The corner of Elizabeth's mouth curved slightly, and for the first time Maria thought she detected a faint trace of hope in her friend's expression. "I'm sorry too, you know," she told Elizabeth before exhaling sharply and shaking her head. "I just can't believe we let a jerk like Conner McDermott come between us."

Elizabeth looked down at the floor, and Maria sensed she had said something wrong. "You still care about him, don't you?" she asked, searching her friend's face. Elizabeth's small nod was almost imperceptible. Before Maria could decide whether she felt bad for Elizabeth or resentful that Conner was still important to her, the door to the *Oracle* office whipped open.

"Hey, Lizzie. I thought I'd—oh." Jessica stopped abruptly when she saw Maria. "Sorry. I can come back later," she said, beginning to back out of the room.

"That's okay," Maria said. "I was getting ready to leave anyway. We're cool, right?" She looked at Elizabeth for confirmation and received a smile. It was a weak one, but Maria guessed it was about all Elizabeth had the energy for right now. She leaned over and hugged her friend, relief flooding through her as Elizabeth hugged her back. "So I'll talk to you later?" Maria asked.

"Definitely," Elizabeth answered over Maria's shoulder.

Maria stood and smiled quickly at Elizabeth, then turned and grinned at Jessica on her way out the door so Jessica would know everything had gone all right. As Maria started down the hall toward her locker, she felt like a huge weight had been lifted.

She knew all the wounds weren't healed, but she and Elizabeth were on the mend. She allowed herself a private little smile. She was glad she'd been the one to come forward and try to fix things. It felt good to be the bigger person.

Angel rang the doorbell at Tia's for the second time. He could tell she was inside playing some kind of game with her brothers, and it was pretty obvious they weren't going to hear the doorbell over their yelling and cheering. Finally he just pushed open the door and walked in.

"Hey, baby," Tia yelled as he entered the living room. She and her brothers were huddled in front of the television, and Tia was holding a controller and maneuvering wildly.

Tomás ran over and jumped into Angel's arms. "Tia just made it to level ten!" he shouted enthusiastically, wrapping his arms around Angel's neck.

Angel grabbed Tomás under his knees and hung him upside down, causing Tomás to screech with glee. "Your big sister's pretty good, huh?" Angel asked.

Tomás giggled as Angel pulled him back up. "Yeah, she kicked Miguel's butt."

Angel pretended to look shocked. "Tomás! Where did you learn to talk like that?"

"Tia," Tomás answered, smiling devilishly. Angel laughed and put the kid down so that he could take a seat on the couch.

Tia paused the game and set down her controller. "I only said it because it's true," she explained, turning to Angel and grinning. "I *did* kick Miguel's butt."

"Did not!" Miguel said, starting toward her, but Tia stopped him by handing him the controller.

"You can finish my game," she offered, nodding toward the television. Miguel was instantly mesmerized by the screen. Angel marveled at how well Tia handled her brothers. It never ceased to amaze him that she could be their big sister, friend, and babysitter all at once.

Tia put her hands on Angel's shoulders and pulled him in for a kiss.

"Ewww!" taunted Miguel and Jesse.

Tia shot her brothers a sideways glance. "Let's go in the kitchen," she said to Angel, taking him by the hand. Angel followed her silently out of the room, smiling because she couldn't seem to keep her hands off him. When they reached the kitchen, Tia grabbed a mug from one of the cabinets and held it up.

"Sure," Angel answered. He watched as Tia reached for another mug, admiring the way her blue sneakers and short wrap skirt accentuated her flexed calf muscles. As she set the mugs down on the counter, he brushed her thick, freshly curled hair to one side and lightly kissed the back of her neck, causing her to giggle. Tia pulled away temporarily to fill a kettle of water and put it on the stove while Angel scooped cocoa into the mugs. When the preparations were finished, she turned back to Angel and put her arms around his neck. He leaned down automatically to kiss her.

"Thought you had to work late," she whispered, her lips still pressed to his.

Angel straightened up and rested his chin on Tia's head. "It was slow. Mr. Walker let me go early," he answered.

"I'm glad," Tia said, squeezing him tightly and sighing. She broke away, and they sat down at the table. Angel looked at Tia, her large brown eyes full of warmth, and felt for the millionth time that he could look at her forever.

"It's good you stopped by," Tia said, breaking the silence. "There's something I've been meaning to talk to you about."

For no apparent reason, Angel felt himself beginning to tense. "What's that?" he asked, furrowing his brow.

"Our anniversary," Tia chirped, grinning. Angel cringed. He hoped that Tia hadn't noticed. "It's coming up soon," Tia continued, "and I had an idea."

Angel felt almost overcome by a sense of doom. "Yeah?" he asked, trying to sound relaxed. In the past he and Tia had always done something amazing for their anniversary. Amazing and *expensive*. When he was just a high-school student and not so focused on saving, his job at the shop had given him money to burn.

"Well," Tia began, her eyes sparkling, "we've always done something really cool to celebrate, so I was thinking that maybe this year we could take a day trip into San Francisco and do a minicruise around the bay. Then there's this trendy restaurant I've been dying to check out."

"Um . . . yeah, maybe," Angel said, trying to sound excited, but he couldn't help feeling like a cartoon character with dollar signs in his eyes. Exactly how were they supposed to afford this? *It's not like I have a ton of cash lying around anymore*, he thought.

Suddenly Tia's expression changed. "But that was just one idea," she said, hesitating. "And now that I think about it, I'm not sure I want to spend that much time driving. So maybe we could make a romantic dinner at home—like my mom's paella, totally from scratch. It would be fun to cook together, don't you think? And then we could rent a movie or go for a walk in the moonlight . . . whatever. As long as we're together."

Angel squirmed in his seat. Her voice was upbeat enough, but he could see the disappointment on her face. *She's so sweet,* he thought, looking into Tia's apologetic eyes. *And I'm so broke. But how can I disappoint her?*

"You know, baby, I think I liked your first idea better," he said.

Tia's eyebrows shot up. "But Angel, how—"

"Don't worry about it," Angel interrupted her, holding up his hand. "I can afford to splurge a little once in a while." Tia's eyes widened, and she started to smile, but Angel could see she was still a little hesitant. "Trust me," he assured her, "it'll be okay. And we're going to do something great."

The teakettle whistled, and Tia got up from the table to retrieve it. *Just don't ask me how,* Angel thought, staring into his hands.

"Milk, right?" Tia asked, looking back at him.

"You got it," Angel answered. He watched Tia stir the cocoa while he silently tried to figure out how he was going to pay for the amazing anniversary he had just promised her. Between working two jobs, saving for college, and trying not to disappoint his girlfriend, he was really beginning to feel stressed out.

*Maybe I'll die of stress, and then Tia can collect the life insurance and use that money for our anniversary,* he thought. *Too bad I don't have a policy.*

"Can you pass the potatoes, please?" Maria asked, pointing at the bowl next to her father. He lifted the blue-speckled casserole dish and handed it across the table. "Thanks," Maria said, but as she set the bowl next to her plate, Maria noticed her mother was eyeing her.

*What did I do wrong?* she wondered, glancing around the table. Maria blushed when she noticed that her red linen napkin was still folded neatly into its ring. Quickly she placed her napkin in her lap. No sooner had she completed the task than Mrs. Slater went back to the business of scooping vegetables onto her own plate. Maria laughed inwardly at her mother's good manners.

*Frances Slater's first rule of table etiquette: Always put your napkin on your lap before serving yourself,* she mused, her lips curling into a discreet smile. *After seventeen years in this house, nobody will ever accuse me of not knowing which fork to use,* she thought.

"So, honey," her mother began as Maria scooped a spoonful of mashed potatoes onto her plate.

"How's the play coming along? Do you think you'll be ready for opening night?"

"Actually, yeah," Maria answered, replacing the serving spoon in the dish. "And to be truthful, I'm kind of surprised."

"I'm not," Mr. Slater said in a proud tone. "You've always been good under pressure." Maria watched as he and her mother exchanged smiles.

"It's one of your strong points," said Mrs. Slater. Their words caught Maria off guard. She knew they were interested in her work on the play, but this was more than she had hoped for. *They're really proud of me*, she thought, staring down at her plate.

"Well, *I* wasn't sure I could pull it off," Maria said. She started to pick up a piece of fried chicken and then thought better of it. *Frances Slater's second rule of table etiquette: Don't talk with your mouth full.* Maria placed her hands in her lap and fidgeted with her napkin as she spoke. "And technically, I guess I haven't yet," she continued. "I still have to make it through the performance on Saturday without forgetting my lines or getting stage fright or something."

Frances Slater stabbed a honey-glazed carrot with her fork and held it a centimeter above her plate. "I'm sure you have nothing to worry about, dear," she said. "Whether you realize it or not, you're a wonderful actress. You always have been. I'm sure the audience will be dazzled." She smiled warmly at

Maria before gracefully bringing her fork to her mouth. How did her mother make eating elegant?

"Your mother's right, you know," her father added. "You have a natural ability." Maria knew she was grinning foolishly, but she didn't care. It had been so long since her parents had been this excited about anything she was doing—all their praise was almost too much to take.

"Thanks," Maria managed. "Do you really think I'm good?" she asked, half believing that she was about to wake up from a dream.

"You're more than good, Maria," her mother answered. "You're superb."

Maria watched her father nodding. "Wow," she said, looking back and forth between her parents. "You know, everyone in the cast has been telling me that I'm doing a really good job, but I thought they were all just being nice."

Mrs. Slater shrugged. "I'm sure they are being nice to some extent, but they're also being truthful," she said.

Maria was beside herself. *Maybe I really am a natural,* she thought.

"It's just too bad that Nina won't be here to see your play." Mr. Slater shook his head. "I know she'd really love to see you onstage again."

Mrs. Slater nodded, but Maria almost choked on her potatoes. *Maria's number-one rule of table etiquette: Don't bring up Nina when we're discussing me!*

95

"Yeah, that is too bad," Maria managed after she had stopped coughing, but truthfully she was glad Nina would be three thousand miles away on opening night. Maria looked up at her parents and smiled. It would be nice to have her parents focus all their attention on her for one night.

# Jessica Wakefield

Okay. So obviously I'm not returning this journal because I've already written in it. But tomorrow the necklace goes back. I was going to give it back today, but Charlie was absent — probably because he was so embarrassed after the way he kissed me at play rehearsal yesterday. I mean, could he have been less subtle? I almost feel bad for him now. How am I supposed to tell him that I'm not interested without crushing him? Maybe I should just keep the necklace and pretend I don't know who it's from. That way I wouldn't have to hurt his feelings <u>and</u> I'd get to keep the necklace.

It does look good on me.

But I can't do that. It wouldn't be right. Charlie should be able to give it to someone who actually cares about him, and Jeremy deserves a girlfriend who doesn't go around accepting jewelry from other guys. So I guess I have to return it. You know, sometimes I wish I didn't have a conscience.

# CHAPTER 6

## All Work and No Play

"Oh my God. There he is," Jessica said, sitting upright on her chair in the cafeteria. She could feel her hands shaking, and she was starting to think that approaching Charlie in the middle of the crowded lunchroom wasn't such a great idea.

"Well, don't just sit there," Tia said, giving her a little push. "Go get him."

Jessica shuddered. "I'm not so sure I want to anymore."

Elizabeth put her arm around her sister. "You can do it, Jess. Just let him down easy," she said, patting her on the back. Unfortunately Jessica didn't share her sister's confidence.

"Come on, Jess," Maria chimed in. "Just pretend you're onstage. You're playing a part."

Jessica took a deep breath and nodded. "Okay. I can do that," she said, steeling herself. She took the velvet box and stood up shakily.

*It's better to set him straight now than to make him think he's got a shot,* Jessica told herself as she walked over to the lunch line. So why did she feel like the biggest jerk on the planet?

She walked up behind him and swallowed hard. "Hi, Charlie," she said, aware that her voice sounded artificially enthusiastic.

"Jessica." He nodded, taking a step forward as the line progressed.

*He's barely even looking at me,* Jessica thought. *He must be so nervous.*

"Um, this is kind of awkward, so I'm just going to say it," she started. Charlie raised his eyebrows as he studied her eyes. "Okay. You're a great guy, and I'm really flattered by all the attention and everything, but I have a boyfriend." Jessica held the box out to him, but Charlie didn't move. Instead he stared at Jessica as if she had nine heads.

"What are you talking about?" he asked, his expression blank.

Jessica felt her stomach start to shift. "This," she said, tilting the box. "I can't accept it."

Realization spread over Charlie's face, and he smirked. "You think I gave you that?"

Jessica felt all the color wash out of her. She was sure there was a puddle the same shade as her complexion spreading across the linoleum floor. "Um—"

"Get over yourself," Charlie finally said. "It's just a play. It's not like I'm *really* kissing you, you know."

Jessica searched for her power of speech but came up empty. She just stood there, sweating and feeling ridiculously conspicuous. Charlie gave her one more pitying look before he moved forward and grabbed a tray from the cart. Jessica almost whimpered aloud, but somehow she managed to unglue her feet and slink back to her table.

"Well? What happened?" Tia asked as Jessica sat back down.

"What did he say?" Maria demanded.

Jessica just shook her head. "It's not him," she said quietly.

"What?" Tia shouted.

Jessica let her head drop onto the table. "It's not him," she repeated, her voice muffled. "I'm such a major idiot." She felt Elizabeth drape an arm around her and lean close to her head.

"I wouldn't say *major*," Elizabeth said.

"Yeah. More like minor," Tia added.

"Or minorly major," Maria put in, a laugh in her voice.

Jessica groaned. "It's so nice to have friends like you."


"Perfect," Maria said, standing back to study the makeup table in the girls' dressing room.

Over the last week it had become a total clutter zone as people kept bringing in new items they needed for the play. All of the lipsticks, hair sprays, bobby pins, eyeliners, and various forms of stage makeup had nearly taken over the table, but in the last half hour Maria had managed to organize all of it. Now each of the girls had a designated space at the mirror, and since Maria had done the rearranging, she didn't see anything wrong with snagging the best spot—right in the middle.

*This way,* she thought, *we won't have to waste time running around back here between scenes.* As a final touch, she placed a framed photograph in front of the mirror where she would easily be able to see it every time she sat down at her stool. It was a picture of herself at age five in her first big play—a Broadway production of *Annie* in which she had played one of the orphans.

"There," Maria said aloud, pleased with her work. She was still admiring the photo when Sarah Douglass came in. She glanced at the counter and then at Maria, lowering one eyebrow suspiciously.

"Did you do this?" Sarah asked, gesturing at the makeup table.

Maria smiled. "Yeah. What do you think?"

"I think you're taking up more than your share of space," Sarah replied, looking sideways at Maria. She pulled a barrette from her hair, letting her long blond mane fall around her shoulders, and tossed the barrette onto the counter with a clatter.

Maria was dumbstruck. "I was just trying to make things easier," she said.

"Yeah, for yourself," Sarah snapped, dropping her bag on the floor. "What did you do with my stuff?"

"It's—" Maria watched as Sarah found her things and started spreading them out. Thankfully, Jessica and Tia walked in at that moment, and Maria shot them a helpless glance. She knew they'd back her up.

"What's going on?" Jessica asked slowly, looking from Sarah to Maria and back again.

"Our star here just rearranged the whole makeup area so she could sit front and center," Sarah announced, crossing her arms over her vinyl jacket.

Jessica glanced at the counter and knitted her brow. Maria almost panicked. Was she mad too? "I'm sure there's a reason Maria reorganized everything," Jessica told Sarah in a rational tone. Then she turned back to Maria and slowly pushed her blond hair behind her ears. "Isn't there?"

Maria blinked. "Well . . . of—of course there is," she stammered, beginning to feel like she was on trial. "I mean, the table was a total mess—you know that. I just wanted to make it so we could all find our stuff easily between scenes," she explained, combing one hand through her unruly black curls.

"You mean you wanted to make it easier for *yourself*," Sarah said again, rolling her eyes. "Isn't that why all *your* things are in the middle, taking up half the counter?"

Maria scowled at Sarah. *What is wrong with this girl?* she wondered. "No," Maria corrected her, trying not to let her racing heart have an effect on her voice. "I didn't think anyone would really care *where* they were as long as we all had space. But since you mentioned it, I *do* have a lot of costume changes."

Sarah stared flatly at Maria. "We all have the same number of costume changes," she scoffed.

"Yeah, but I have more stage time," Maria answered, forcing herself to speak slowly. "So I have less time to change."

Sarah shook her head and rolled her eyes again. "You are *so*—"

"—right," Tia said quickly, stepping between Maria and Sarah. "You know, I've been looking for this forever," she continued, picking up a brush from the makeup table. "And now that Maria's reorganized everything, I can finally brush my hair again." Tia flashed them both a wide grin and ran the brush through her hair excitedly, as if she'd been looking forward to this moment for months.

Jessica smiled and shook her head at Tia. "You are such a freak," she said, but Tia just happily continued brushing. Sarah sighed, but she headed for the other side of the room. When she was gone, Maria felt her shoulders relax.

"Thanks," Maria whispered to Tia, touching her arm lightly.

"No problem," Tia said. "I'll brush my hair for you anytime," she joked, tossing her head so dramatically that her hair skimmed across Jessica's face.

"Watch it, Rapunzel," Jessica quipped.

Maria smiled. "Hey, thank you too, Jess," she said, lightly elbowing Jessica's arm. "I'm glad you guys came in when you did," she whispered, glancing over at Sarah. "She was really mad at me. What's her problem anyway?" Tia and Jessica just shrugged and looked at each other. "Wait a minute," Maria said, biting her lip, "you guys aren't mad at me, are you?"

Tia looked at Jessica and then at Maria. "No," she said, waving one hand dismissively. "If you hadn't cleaned up, I wouldn't have found my brush."

Jessica groaned. "Would you stop it with the brush already?"

Tia giggled and shook her head, causing her hair to cascade down over her back again. "You're just jealous of my luscious locks."

"What about you, Jess?" Maria asked.

"Of course not," Jessica said, glancing over Maria's shoulder. She leaned closer to Maria and lowered her voice. "Sarah's probably just a little sensitive because she thought she was going to get the lead when she found out Renee couldn't do it."

Maria's eyes widened. "I didn't know that."

"Yeah." Tia nodded, reaching into her bag and pulling out a thick headband. "She tried out for Priscilla. There was major trauma when she didn't get it. Crying in the bathroom and everything."

"And the picture starts to come into focus," Maria said, stealing a glance at Sarah in the mirror. So Sarah was jealous. *That* Maria could handle. She took a deep breath and sat down at the center of the vanity, running her hands along its smooth surface. *I knew I hadn't done anything wrong.*

"Dammit!" Angel muttered under his breath. "I just had it two seconds ago." He patted his gray coveralls, but they were empty—minus the grease-covered cloth hanging from his back pocket. After rifling through the red, metal toolbox and scanning the top of his dad's workbench, Angel was just about ready to explode. There was no sign of the socket wrench anywhere.

*If I could just find the damn thing, I could finish up and go home,* he thought, pawing through the toolbox one more time. "Then I might actually get to shower between jobs," he grumbled, looking at his hands. They were covered with oil and dirt from working at the garage all day, and he had to be at the Riot in a little over an hour for the dinner shift.

"Uuughh!" Angel yelled, standing up and clearing all the tools off the workbench with one long sweep of his arms. He watched as boxes of bolts and screws tumbled to the ground around him with a tremendous clatter. In a matter of seconds everything was silent again except for the tinny noise of a hubcap rolling across the concrete floor.

Angel buried his hands in his short, black hair, aware that he was getting grease all over himself but past the point of caring. In a final burst of energy he stepped closer to one of the steel tool cabinets and kicked it hard with his right foot. "Why does everything always go down at once?" he murmured, looking at the floor and shaking his head.

"When it rains, it pours," a voice called through the open garage door.

Angel looked up to see Conner in the doorway. "How long have you been standing there, man?" he asked, hoping Conner hadn't witnessed his tantrum.

"Long enough," Conner answered, entering the garage and walking over to Angel. "What's up?" he asked, taking a seat at the makeshift desk where Angel's dad calculated bills and ordered parts.

"Nothing," Angel said quickly. "I just can't find the socket wrench I need to finish this job and get out of here." Conner nodded in understanding. "Nine millimeter?" he asked.

Angel narrowed his eyes. "Yeah. How did—" He stopped midsentence to see the exact wrench he had been looking for in Conner's outstretched hand. Angel took it from Conner's grip and stared at it.

"It was on the desk," Conner said plainly. Angel felt like a compete jerk. He rolled his eyes and looked up at the ceiling, almost embarrassed to meet Conner's gaze. "So what's really going on?" Conner asked, pushing off the desk with his legs and letting the chair roll back to the center of the garage.

"Just the usual," Angel said, shrugging. "You know—not enough money, not enough time. That kind of stuff." Conner just nodded, and Angel remembered how easy it was to talk to him, even though it had been a long time since they'd hung out together without Tia there too. Conner was cool. Once he had accepted you as a friend, he never judged, he never twisted conversations to focus on his own problems, and he never repeated anything to anyone. He just listened. "Sorry about the drama show," Angel apologized, gesturing at all the tools strewn about the floor.

Conner chuckled as he wheeled his chair back to the desk. "You know what you need?" he asked, raising one eyebrow.

"What?" Angel asked.

"You need to take a night off and hang with the guys," Conner answered with a grin.

*Yeah, right,* Angel thought. *I can hear it now. "No, I don't have to work tonight, Tia, I just thought I'd blow you off so I could go out with some friends."*

"I don't know, man," Angel said, shifting his weight from one foot to the other. "I don't exactly have free time to spare."

"That's the point," Conner said. "You need to *make* some." Angel squinted thoughtfully as he took in his friend's words. Conner leveled him with his penetrating green-eyed stare. "Tia's cool. She'll understand."

Angel shook his head and slid his hands into his pockets. "That obvious, huh?" he asked. Conner lifted one shoulder and smirked. "Well, maybe you're right. It would be nice to just forget about everything for a few hours."

"Now you're talking," Conner said.

Angel narrowed his eyes at Conner suspiciously. "You sure *you're* not the one who needs it?" he asked. He knew Conner had been under some stress himself lately, even if he never talked about it.

"Does it matter?" Conner asked indifferently.

Angel smiled. "I guess not," he said, bending down to pick up some of the tools. "I was just wondering how things were at the McDermott-Sandborn homestead."

Conner exhaled sharply through his nose. "Well, Megan's still not talking to me because of Elizabeth, and I'm not sure my mom has even noticed Elizabeth is missing, and—"

Angel looked up as Conner stopped abruptly and noticed a distinct blush rising to his friend's cheeks. He knew Conner had just said more than he wanted to.

"So, about this night out," Angel said. "What do you have in mind?"

Conner stood and started collecting the nuts and bolts that were scattered around the floor, placing them in a plastic bucket. "Nothing yet," he answered, "but I'll make a few calls and see what I can come up with. Just keep Friday night open."

"I'm already there," Angel answered, glancing up at the clock. He was down to fifty minutes until his shift started at the Riot. *If I live that long,* he thought.

# Conner McDermott

There's something to be said for guys who are real <u>guys.</u> Just ask John Wayne, Humphrey Bogart, or Marlon Brando—they all knew it. Their characters were men of few words who didn't waste time with small talk. And they were always in charge. They never let anyone in, and they never apologized.

That's the way it should be with guys. That's the way it should be, period.

# CHAPTER
## A Little Tense

**7**

"Just act natural," Ken muttered to himself, wondering if he still knew how.

When he had first sat down, Maria was the only one there, and Ken had figured he was comfortable enough with her to share a lunch table. But in a matter of moments Tia and Jessica had arrived, then Elizabeth, and a few seconds later Andy, another one of Maria's new friends. Now, as he looked around the table, Ken was starting to feel a little claustrophobic.

*Only twenty more minutes,* he thought, looking at his watch. *If I can smile and nod for twenty more minutes, they might actually think I'm normal.* Ken was surprised to find that he actually cared what Maria's friends thought of him. It had been a while since he'd cared what anyone thought about anything.

"I'll be so embarrassed if I mess up that line on opening night," Tia was saying. "And it will be totally your fault," she added, pointing at Jessica.

"My fault?" Jessica asked, looking confused.

"What am I, a ventriloquist putting words in your mouth?"

"I guess that makes you the dummy, Tee," Andy said.

Tia smacked Andy's arm and scowled. "As if," she said before turning back to Jessica. "It'll be your fault because you're the one who made me so self-conscious about it. Now every time I get to that part, I start giggling like an idiot—and it's supposed to be a serious scene!"

Jessica laughed. "I can't help it if you have a sick sense of humor," she said innocently. Tia threw a potato chip at her, and Andy started applauding.

"You two put on a great show," he said, "but I have a question. Can Tia talk if you drink a glass of water?" he asked, pointing at Jessica.

"No, but my arms still work," Tia answered, wrapping her hands around Andy's neck and pretending to choke him. Andy lolled his head to one side, rolled back his eyes, and stuck out his tongue. He looked so ridiculous that even Elizabeth, who had been pretty subdued, laughed out loud.

Ken had to chuckle too. He was starting to think he didn't have to worry so much about hanging out with Maria and her friends. They were all pretty easygoing. *And for a change, I'm not even the quietest one in the group,* he thought, glancing at Elizabeth. Then, searching the cafeteria, Ken began to wonder if maybe the ever-elusive Conner would be joining them too. He would have liked to meet the guy that had Maria and Elizabeth so torqued. But unless Conner was either incredibly brave or stupid, he probably wouldn't sit down at a table with both girls present.

Finally Tia released Andy, shaking her head and scowling at him. Andy grimaced and started rubbing his neck. "Ouch," he said with a groan. "I think you really hurt me, Tee. Not bad for a puppet," he finished, smiling, and ducked just in time to dodge the balled-up napkin Tia had thrown at him.

"Anyway, Tee," Jessica said when their laughter had subsided. "Don't worry about the line. If you forget it, I'll just say it for you. I'm better than you are anyway."

Tia was about to launch a verbal assault on Jessica when Maria's sober tone stopped them. "You guys are kidding, right?" Maria asked.

"About what?" Jessica returned.

Maria smiled. "About missing lines or laughing in the middle of the play." Maria looked directly at Tia. "If you really think you're going to have a problem, maybe I can work with you this afternoon and give you some tips I learned when I was little."

Tia started to laugh but then seemed to realize that Maria was dead serious. Tia glanced at Jessica, who just raised her eyebrows. No one seemed to know what to say.

"I bet that's been really helpful to you," Ken

jumped in, speaking to Maria. "I mean, having all that experience from before must have made it easier for you to get ready for the play so—so quickly," he stammered.

Maria nodded. "Actually, yeah," she answered. "I worked with some really great actors, and I've used a lot of what they taught me during the last week. In fact," she said, looking back at Jessica and Tia again, "I've been meaning to talk to you guys about your projection. I don't think Ms. Delaney's noticed because she's been standing right next to the stage, but I was in the back of the auditorium during the second diner scene yesterday, and your voices just aren't carrying."

Jessica and Tia glanced at each other and then at Maria.

"Really," Tia stated. Jessica leaned back and crossed her arms over her chest.

"Mm-hmm." Maria nodded, finishing a bite of her yogurt. "But I've got some simple voice exercises I can show you this afternoon that will really help."

"Great," Jessica said dryly. "Thanks." She began moving her salad around her plate with her fork while Tia bit into a french fry and stared up at the ceiling. Ken glanced at Andy, half panicked, wishing there was something he could say or do to end the awkward silence.

"You know," Andy began, looking at Ken, "I've known Tia for a long time, and I've got to say, I have

116

a hard time thinking of her as 'not loud enough.'"
Tia glared at him, but Jessica chuckled.

"I know what you mean," Elizabeth said, nodding. "I've never had trouble hearing Jessica either."

"Hey," Jessica protested, shooting her sister a sinister look.

*That's better,* Ken thought, feeling the tension ease a little.

"Yeah, it's weird," Maria agreed. "But even typically loud voices can take on a totally different tonal quality onstage." Ken flinched as he noticed Jessica and Tia stiffening in their seats. *Oh, no,* he thought, cradling his head in one hand and glancing over at Andy. *Here we go again.*

"Hey, I've got an acting issue I need help with," Andy said out of the blue. Ken looked over at Andy hopefully. He couldn't tell if Andy was serious or just kidding around, but at this point any conversation seemed welcome.

"Yeah?" Maria asked immediately, her eyes brightening.

"Well, I don't want to mention any names or anything," Andy started, "but a couple of my friends—Tia and Jessica—keep talking to me about this play they're in, and I was wondering if you could tell me how to pretend I care," he finished in perfect deadpan.

"Andy!" Tia and Jessica yelled in unison. Andy started laughing, and in a matter of seconds Jessica, Tia, Liz, and even Maria had joined in.

Andy glanced over at Ken, and Ken smiled back. *He's okay,* Ken thought, chuckling to himself. *In fact, he's pretty cool.*

"Can you *believe* Maria?" Jessica asked, sifting through the pile of books in her locker. "It's, like, 'Hi! I know everything!'"

"Seriously," Tia grumbled, leaning back against the locker next to Jessica's. "I should have been strangling her instead of Andy."

Elizabeth frowned. "C'mon, you guys. It wasn't *that* bad."

"Are you kidding?" Jessica asked, yanking her French book free from the stack. "It's like she thinks she's the diva of SVH." She pulled out a notebook, and a red envelope fluttered to the floor.

"Oh my God. It's another one!" Jessica blurted out, her blue-green eyes wide.

"Are you going to pick it up?" Tia asked.

Jessica grabbed the envelope and shakily ripped it open. She glanced at the small card. "It says, 'See you Sunday night, 7 P.M., gate B,' with a question mark," Jessica read. She held it out for Tia and her sister to see.

"What's that supposed to mean?" Elizabeth asked, frowning as she straightened her cropped blue cardigan over the waist of her twill miniskirt.

Jessica looked into the envelope and pulled out two slips of paper. Tickets. Her heart pounded as she read the information printed on them. "I don't believe it." She held up the tickets. "They're for that benefit concert at the coliseum on Sunday," she said, smiling. "I heard about it on the radio. This is so cool!" She fluttered the tickets in front of their faces.

"It's definitely cool," Elizabeth said, hesitating, "but aren't you a little nervous?"

"About what?" Jessica asked, blinking.

"About finally meeting Mr. Wonderful," Tia interjected, pointing at the card.

Elizabeth nodded. "Yeah. What if he's some weirdo or something?"

Jessica recoiled at her sister's words. "Oh my God, you're right," she said. She fingered the tickets in her hand. "He could be a total stalker."

All of a sudden she was acutely aware of all the people passing by. She felt like everyone was staring at her. "Or what if this is all a big joke?" she asked, lowering her voice. "I mean, what if someone's just setting me up to look like an idiot?" Jessica shuddered as she glanced over her shoulder.

"I'm sure it's not a joke, Jess," Elizabeth said. "Whoever it is obviously likes you. He's left you some pretty nice things." She gestured at the tickets. "Those aren't cheap, you know. I doubt someone gave them to you as a prank."

Jessica shrugged. "I guess. But still, what if he's a freak?"

Tia laughed. "Don't worry about it," she said, pulling a piece of string off the skirt of her bright red tank dress. "There's a simple solution."

"Yeah?" Jessica asked, squinting hopefully. "Do I still get to see the concert?"

Tia shook her head. "That's what I like about you, Jess," she said. "You've always got your priorities in order."

Elizabeth chuckled.

"Thank you," Jessica said sweetly, accepting Tia's gibe as a compliment. "So what's your plan?"

"It's easy," Tia said. "Elizabeth and I will go with you to the concert, and we'll wait outside until your stalker—I mean *secret admirer*—shows up. That way you don't have to be alone with him. If he's a sicko, we can easily ditch him. I drive a mean getaway car."

"That's perfect," Jessica said, heaving a sigh of relief.

"What have you ever had to get away from?" Elizabeth asked Tia.

Tia smiled mischievously. "There are things about me you will never know."

"Yeah, right," Jessica said sarcastically. "Are you up for an outing with us on Sunday, Liz?" she asked, even though she had no intention of letting Elizabeth say no.

"I don't have any other plans," Elizabeth answered, lifting one shoulder.

"Great!" Jessica responded, barely able to contain

her excitement. In just three days she was going to find out who this mystery man was. And then, of course, she was going to have to do the "letting him down gently" thing again. She thought back to her confrontation with Charlie. Maybe she should practice a little before Sunday.

*Finally,* Maria thought as the last bell rang. She jumped from her seat and headed for the door like a sprinter in the hundred-meter dash. French class had dragged on forever. There were only two more days until opening night, and all Maria could think about was the play. She wished she could just skip her Friday classes and spend the time rehearsing instead. It wasn't like she could concentrate on anything else anyway.

She was just about to clear the door and start down the hall when she heard someone call her name. *Not now,* she thought, turning around to see who it was.

"Maria, I'm glad I caught you," Elizabeth said, catching up.

"Hey, Liz," Maria said, trying not to sound irritated. It wasn't that she didn't want to talk to Elizabeth—she just didn't want anything to make her late for rehearsal.

"Do you have a minute?" Elizabeth asked tentatively.

"Actually, no," Maria said, smiling apologetically.

She continued down the hallway with Elizabeth scurrying along beside her. "I really need to get to rehearsal. It's our first full-dress run-through, and if I'm late, it will throw everybody off."

"Oh," Elizabeth said, looking surprised.

Maria sped up her pace. *I need to remember to tell Ms. Delaney how hard it is to hear everyone from the back of the auditorium,* she thought. Then she realized that Elizabeth was still talking.

"I'm sorry, what?" Maria asked, stopping and turning to face her friend.

"I just need to talk to you for a second," Elizabeth said.

Maria took a deep breath. "Can it wait?" she asked hopefully. "I really need to be on time. They can't start without me. My character's in most of the scenes, and I've been helping with some of the direction too." She searched Elizabeth's face for some sign of understanding.

"It's kind of important," Elizabeth said, hugging her books to her chest. "I promise it won't take long."

Maria sighed and checked her watch. "Okay," she said finally, forcing herself to smile. "I guess I still have a few minutes before I officially have to be down there."

"It's about the newspaper," Elizabeth started. "I know I haven't been around much, so I was thinking—"

*Oh my God,* Maria thought, tuning out the rest of Elizabeth's sentence. *I left my costume for act two in my locker.*

"I'm sorry, Liz," Maria interrupted. "I really have to go. Can we do this later?" Elizabeth looked confused, but before she had a chance to respond, Maria took off down the hallway.

If she hurried, she could get changed and still have time to run her ideas past Ms. Delaney. *And I have to make a mental note to call Liz later,* she thought, realizing Elizabeth had seemed a little upset. *I wonder what Conner did this time.*

# Ken Matthews

Mr. Ford handed back our history essays today, and instead of the usual "see me after class" comment, I actually got a B on mine. I showed it to Maria, and she was pretty psyched. She should be. She deserves all the credit for it. I never would have even finished it if she hadn't badgered me in the first place. Now I finally have a grade that I don't have to hide from my parents.

Then today at lunch I actually sat around and talked with other people. I used to think I'd never wanted to hang out with anyone again, but Maria's friends are pretty cool, and besides, no one's talking about the earthquake anymore. Ever since Maria and I started talking, getting out of bed in the morning hasn't seemed like such a bad thing.

Maybe I should figure out a way to thank her.

"If she tells me I missed my mark one more time, I'm gonna hit *her* mark," Tia muttered to Jessica.

Jessica nodded. "I know what you mean," she whispered back. "I think we've created a monster." The two girls were standing at center stage while Maria stood on the floor next to Ms. Delaney, making suggestions about the positioning of the various cast members in the scene.

"I know you probably blocked all of this out in the first two weeks," Tia heard Maria say, "but when I was reading through the play last night, it hit me that this scene would flow a lot easier if we brought Jessica and Tia in from the left and had them exit stage right."

"Interesting," Ms. Delaney said, studying the stage. Tia heard it, but she couldn't believe it. She had expected Ms. Delaney to put an end to Maria's constant comments and critiques over an hour ago, but the more Maria talked, the more impressed Ms. Delaney seemed. *This is making me physically ill,* Tia thought.

"Girls," Ms. Delaney called. "Why don't you try it again and enter from the left, as Maria suggested?"

Tia nodded and picked up the hemline of her evening gown, shuffling offstage behind Jessica. "I'm gonna vomit," she whispered to Jessica's back. "What does Maria think she's doing?"

"Shhh! Keep your voice down," Jessica said as they positioned themselves and waited for their cue.

"Don't tell me this isn't bothering you," Tia said incredulously.

"Not at all," Jessica replied. "I *love* to be bossed around by someone who's only been in the cast for six days and thinks she's the reigning queen of Broadway."

Tia sighed. "So I'm not crazy. For a second I was beginning to think I was the only one."

"Are you kidding?" Jessica whispered. "Why do you think half the cast is currently taking an unscheduled break?" Tia peeked out at the auditorium. Sure enough, the seats were empty. The few cast members in the scene were the only ones around, and they were all hanging out in the wings.

Tia ducked back behind the curtain. "Whoa," she said. "I didn't even notice."

Jessica nodded and gingerly adjusted her heavily sprayed hair. "Most of them walked out twenty minutes ago when Miss Demanding decided to play actor-producer-director-and-lighting crew."

Tia chuckled. "What's her deal anyway?" she asked. Before Jessica could comment, they were interrupted by Ms. Delaney's voice.

"Girls! That's your cue!"

Jessica looked at Tia and squared her shoulders. "Come on, Sophie," she said in her husky stage voice. "Let's act."

"Right behind you, Sadie," Tia replied in her character's English accent. "Wouldn't want to upset our star."

Ken scribbled in his notebook, trying to make sense of the jumbled calculus equation in front of him. *Maybe Maria would consider tutoring me in math too,* he mused, looking up at the stage, where play rehearsal was in progress.

He had been alternately watching the rehearsal and working on his math while he waited for Maria to finish up. Her car was in the shop again, and Ken had offered to give her a ride home.

"Ooh, calculus homework, huh?"

Ken looked up as Andy slid into a seat in the row behind him.

"Yeah, it sucks," Ken answered. "I've been on number eight for the last half hour. It's impossible."

"Wait a minute," Andy said, stepping over the row of seats and sitting next to Ken. He leaned over to look at Ken's notebook and then pointed at one of the lines in Ken's calculations.

"That's right," he said, tapping the paper with his index finger, "but in the next line, where it says $f(x)$, you have to go back to the original equation and substitute the whole thing right in there."

"Oh," Ken said, seeing where he'd gone wrong.

"Then you can divide the whole thing by pi and solve for $y$," Andy finished.

Ken shook his head. "I can't believe I didn't see that," he said, exasperated.

"Yeah. That's why I run all my calculus homework past Liz. If I wait till I get home and do it alone, I'm totally lost," Andy replied, leaning against the seat in front of him.

"I know what you mean," Ken said, finishing up his assignment and closing his notebook. "Hey, thanks, man," he said, turning to face Andy. "You just saved me from a night of total frustration." *More like a day of humiliation when I showed up for class tomorrow without my homework. Again,* Ken thought.

"No problem," Andy answered. "We intro-to-calc guys have to stick together," he joked in a fake macho voice.

Ken smiled. The more he got to know Andy, the more he liked him. It was nice to talk to a guy outside of the macho jock crowd he used to hang with.

Unlike his old "friends," Andy had a personality.

"We should get together and study for the midterm that's coming up," Andy suggested.

"I can use all the help I can get," Ken said, nodding.

"Hey, speaking of getting together," Andy said, snapping his fingers, "a couple of the guys and I are hanging out Friday night. You want to come?"

Ken's chest automatically tightened as it always did when the idea of socializing came up.

"Uh, are you having a party or s-something?" he stammered, stalling so he could think of an appropriate excuse not to go.

"Nah," Andy answered, shaking his head. "It's just gonna be me, Conner, maybe one of Conner's buddies, and Angel, Tia's boyfriend. Have you met him?"

"No," Ken replied.

"Oh, well, he's really cool. He's a lot like Tia, only bigger and less loud."

Ken laughed despite himself. "Actually, I haven't met Conner either," he added. The idea of finally meeting Maria's major crush was intriguing. *It might be worth going just for that,* Ken thought.

"You haven't?" Andy asked, obviously surprised. "Then you should definitely come. Conner's a laugh a minute," he said sarcastically.

Ken smirked. "What are you guys doing?" he asked.

"*That* I don't know," Andy answered. "Conner's

supposed to come up with something and then e-mail me tonight."

Ken nodded and looked up at the stage. Maybe they'd go see a movie or do something else that wouldn't require much effort.

"Why don't I get your e-mail address and I'll forward it to you? Then you can let me know tomorrow if you want to come," Andy suggested.

"Sure," Ken answered, tearing off a strip of paper and jotting down his e-mail address. He handed it to Andy, who glanced at it and tucked it into his pocket.

Ken sighed, relieved that he didn't have to make a decision right away. With a night to think it over, he could come up with an excuse for not going that wouldn't make him sound like a loser. *Or maybe,* Ken thought, *I'll be able to convince myself to go.*

"I'm so excited!" Maria said, grinning.

"Really?" Ken joked. "I didn't think you were serious the last four times you said that."

Maria shot him a surprised look. "I think you've been hanging around Andy too much. You're beginning to sound like him."

Ken smiled.

*I think he took that as a compliment,* Maria thought.

As they rounded the last corner before Maria's

house, Ken slowed the car to a crawl even Maria's parents would approve of. Then, turning the wheel, he glided into her driveway without any of the jerky braking Maria typically associated with teenage male drivers.

As soon as the car was stopped, Maria started fidgeting with the door handle, anxious to get out and hurry inside. She had already hopped out and run around the car before she realized Ken wasn't doing the same.

"Aren't you coming?" she asked, looking back at him expectantly.

Ken stared up at her through his open window. "You sure you want me to come in? Don't you want to do this by yourself?"

"No way," Maria answered, opening his door for him and taking his hand. "I want a witness." She pulled him from the car, and Ken chuckled as Maria dragged him toward the house.

"All right," he said. "I'm coming." Maria dropped his hand and pushed open the front door. As she crossed the threshold, she fished an envelope out of her bag and then dropped the rest of her belongings on a wooden bench in the foyer.

"Mom! Dad!" she called, running toward the living room excitedly. Maria heard Ken's steady footfalls behind her and grinned, glad that he was here to share this moment with her.

"Maria!" her mother shouted as she entered

the living room. Mrs. Slater walked toward her daughter with outstretched arms. Maria stopped in her tracks. Her parents didn't know why she was so excited, so she wasn't expecting this kind of reception.

She hugged her mother warily and glanced over at her father, who was grinning from ear to ear. Maria's shoulders tensed.

"We have wonderful news!" Mrs. Slater gushed, releasing Maria from her embrace. "Oh, hello, Ken," she said warmly, looking over Maria's shoulder. "Come in."

Ken smiled politely and entered the room. He looked slightly ill at ease, and for once Maria shared his discomfort.

"We just got off the phone with Nina," Mrs. Slater announced. Maria's entire body went rigid at the mention of her sister's name. "She's won a Presidential Scholarship. Brown only awards two each year," Mrs. Slater continued, beaming. "And we're flying out to Rhode Island to accept it with her this weekend! Isn't that wonderful?"

Maria felt all the energy drain out of her. "But what about my play?" she asked quietly, holding up the envelope. "I bought you tickets." Mr. Slater's eyebrows shot up. *They forgot all about it*, Maria thought.

"Well, we can have someone videotape it," her father suggested. "What about you, Ken?" he asked hopefully. Maria slowly turned her head to look at Ken.

Ken glanced over at Maria and then down at his hands. "Um, I'm not so good with cameras," he said.

"Well, I'm sure we can find someone," Mrs. Slater answered, waving a hand. "The point is, Nina's scholarship is a once-in-a-lifetime event," she said, looking sympathetically into Maria's eyes. "You'll certainly have other plays, dear," she said, touching her daughter's shoulder. "In fact, you'll probably be in the spring production, right?"

Maria didn't know how to respond. Realizing she was still holding out the envelope, she withdrew her hand and stuffed it into the pocket of her cargo pants.

"Yeah," she said, nodding slowly. Maria turned and started to leave the room, her mind a complete blur and her insides a complete jumble.

"Are you all right, Maria?" she heard her father call after her.

"I'm fine," she murmured, starting up the stairs to her room on shaky legs.

"Maria?"

She paused midstep at the sound of Ken's voice and turned around slowly. He was standing at the bottom of the stairs, his hands shoved into the pockets of his denim jacket, his eyes full of pity. Maria's vision blurred with unshed tears.

"Maria—," Ken repeated.

"I can't . . . I can't right now, Ken," she said, taking a deep breath. "Just go home."

Then she turned and jogged up the rest of the stairs.

*What was I thinking anyway?* she thought, closing her bedroom door behind her. *Maybe they'd care if I was back in Hollywood working on something* important. *But did I really think a rinky-dink school play would matter?*

# Andy Marsden

**From:** marsden1@swiftnet.com
**To:** kenQB@swiftnet.com
**Time:** 9:10 P.M.
**Subject:** fwd: How 'bout them horses?

Ken,
   Conner's e-mail is below, but since you don't know him, I thought I'd elaborate. He's a man of few words, most of them monosyllabic. ;-)
   Anyway, the plan is to meet at the garage where Angel works around seven-fifteen, and then head over to the racetrack in Big Mesa. I've never been, but Conner's dad used to take him when he was a kid, and he seems to think it'll be fun. We're just going to hang out and watch the races, or, as he put it, "soak up the atmosphere."

                Let me know,
                Andy


From: mcdermott@cal.rr.com
To: marsden1@swiftnet.com
Time:8:32 P.M.
Subject:How 'bout them horses?

   A.—
   Racetrack
   7:30 tomorrow night
   Bring $
   Meet at the garage
   —C.

Maria plodded down the staircase and headed for the front door. She wasn't in the mood for breakfast or her parents this morning. She just wanted to slip out unnoticed. *Unnoticed. That's a laugh. Have I ever actually been noticed in this house?* she thought bitterly.

She stepped outside and started to swing the door closed behind her, but it stuck on something. When Maria turned around, she was surprised to see her father holding the door and her mother standing next to him with her arms crossed.

"Maria, we want to talk with you for a moment," Mrs. Slater said.

Maria rolled her eyes and stepped back inside. *Just what I need right now,* she thought. *More good news from Mom and Dad.* "Why?" she asked indignantly. "Did Nina just win another scholarship or something?"

Her father frowned. "Don't be petulant, Maria," he said in a steady voice. "Your mother and I know you're upset about the play, but you can't go on behaving like a child. You should be happy for your sister, not jealous."

Maria glared at her parents. "That's it!" she yelled vehemently, dropping her book bag to the floor and causing her mother to step back.

Her father's features tightened. "*Maria Frances Slater,*" he bellowed. "Watch your tone!"

"No," Maria barked, shaking her head indignantly. "I've had it. I'm not *jealous* of anything Nina does," she snapped, her hand cutting through the air in a sweeping gesture. "In case you haven't noticed, which I know you haven't, I'm just as smart and talented as she is. I get straight A's, I've been on the honor roll since fourth grade, and I'm probably going to be the valedictorian of my class! And now," she continued, tears welling up in her eyes, "I've got the lead in a play that's really important to me, but you're just blowing it off. For *Nina.* Big surprise there, huh?" she finished, wiping at the corner of her eyes with the back of her hand.

"Maria," her mother said tersely, touching her daughter's shoulder, but Maria pulled away. She grabbed her bag and started out the door again. Her father was mumbling something about being disrespectful, but Maria didn't want to hear it.

"Have fun at Brown," she snapped. And with that, she walked out and slammed the door behind her.

*     *     *

*Are you okay?*

Ken folded the piece of paper in front of him into a neat square and flipped it onto Maria's desk. He watched her out of the corner of his eye while trying to appear as if he was still listening to Mr. Ford's lecture on the United States's role in World War II.

Thirty seconds later Maria tossed the note back to Ken without even glancing in his direction. Ken unfolded it quietly.

*Are you okay?*

*I'm Fine*

The writing was steady, but Ken wasn't so certain about Maria.

*Are you okay?*

*I'm Fine*

*Are you sure?*

He threw the paper onto her desk again, and this time Maria managed to get the note back to him in just fifteen seconds.

*Are you okay?*

*I'm Fine*
====

*Are you sure?*

Ken sighed, crumpled the paper into a tight ball, and copied down the assignment Mr. Ford was writing on the board.

When he had finished, Ken looked over at Maria again. She had already packed up her things and wasn't even bothering to write down the homework.

Okay, she was definitely upset. Majorly upset.

And after the bomb her parents had dropped on her the day before, Ken wasn't surprised. She had been so excited about giving them their tickets, and her parents had completely crushed her.

Ken watched anxiously as the second hand counted down the last minute of class. When the bell rang, he scooped up his notebook, slung his backpack over his shoulder, and raced up the aisle, intent on intercepting his friend.

"Maria! Hey, Maria!" he called as she booked out of class. She didn't turn around. She didn't even flinch. By the time Ken reached the door, Maria was already on her way down the hall, and short of tackling her, Ken was pretty sure he wasn't going to get her to stop and talk to him.

*Maybe she's just not ready to talk about it yet,* he thought, watching her disappear around the corner. He let out a deep, frustrated sigh. *Funny. Didn't I do this to her just a couple of weeks ago?*

"Maria, it's your line," Ms. Delaney called.

Maria closed her eyes and thought, but her mind was a blank. "I'm sorry," she apologized. "Can you give me the lead-in?"

A student sitting in the front row looked up at her and whispered, "That's the way Sadie is."

Maria nodded and looked back at Charlie Rucker. "That's the way Sadie is," she repeated, racking her brain to come up with the rest of the line. "She can walk into any room and instantly become the center of attention." Maria hesitated. "It's always been that way?" she guessed.

The prompter shook his head. "Ever since we were children," he whispered, but this time the line didn't jar Maria's memory at all.

"I'm sorry," she said again, bringing her hand to her forehead and looking at Ms. Delaney helplessly.

"That's all right," Ms. Delaney said as she

approached the stage. "Okay, everyone, let's take a break," she called in a much louder voice. "You can all get changed, and then we'll meet back here. I have some last-minute notes I want to go over before we call it a night." She clapped, and instantly everyone but Maria left the stage.

*Oh, boy,* Maria thought. *They all know she's about to chew me out for doing such a crappy job, and no one wants to get caught in the cross fire.* But as Ms. Delaney approached, Maria noticed that her expression was one of concern, not confrontation.

"Are you all right, Maria?" she asked, her forehead creased with worry lines. "You've done wonderfully all week, but today you seem a bit preoccupied. Is there a problem?"

*Yeah, I'm a total loser, and it's no wonder my parents prefer my sister,* Maria thought. "Not really," she lied. "I'm just kind of tired—I didn't sleep well last night."

Ms. Delaney nodded, but she was still scrutinizing Maria's face.

"Plus I think I've got some preperformance jitters going on," Maria added.

"Ahh," said Ms. Delaney, nodding. "I can relate to that."

Maria shifted her weight from one foot to the other and sighed.

"You're fabulous in this role, Maria," Ms. Delaney said confidently. "And I know you'll be wonderful onstage tomorrow night, so don't worry. All right?"

"All right," Maria said, trying to sound convincing.

"Good," Ms. Delaney said, clapping as though she had just given a pep talk to the entire cast. "Now, go ahead and get changed."

Maria nodded and walked slowly toward the dressing room. *At least it will feel good to get out of this poofy prom dress,* she thought, lifting the skirt of her red taffeta gown. As she opened the door, Jessica and Tia were on their way out. They were still in the matching gold lamé halter dresses their characters had to wear for the office party in the last scene of the play.

"Maria," Jessica said, her voice soft. "We were just coming to check on you. Are you okay?" Maria cringed as she felt Jessica's hand on her back.

"Yeah, you seem a little out of it," Tia added. "Is there something wrong? Do you want to talk about it?"

*I'd be fine if everyone would just back off and stop asking me if I'm okay,* Maria thought. "I just want to be alone," she muttered, trying to walk past them into the dressing room. Unfortunately Tia was blocking the door.

"Are you sure?" Tia asked.

"Is there anything we can do?" Jessica said almost simultaneously.

Maria rolled her eyes and sighed. "What part of *alone* did you misunderstand?" she snapped, walking the other way. Maybe she could find some privacy in the bathroom.

"Hey!" Tia snapped.

Maria sighed and reluctantly turned around.

Tia had both hands on her hips, and her eyes were hard. "We've been putting up with this prima-donna attitude from you all week, and I can't take it anymore. You are *not* the only person in this play."

Maria dropped her jaw, too stunned to speak. What was Tia talking about?

"Get over yourself, Tia. Contrary to your own be-lief, you don't know everything," Maria said. She turned on her heel, hot, angry tears stinging her eyes, and continued on her way out to the bath-room.

"I don't think Tia's the one with the ego prob-lem!" Jessica yelled after her, but Maria just shook her head and kept going. She didn't want them to see her cry. But she'd only walked about twenty feet when Ken rounded the corner and bumped into her.

"Uh, sorry," he said, smiling. "I was just coming to see you." Maria crossed her arms over her chest and stared at him.

"I'm exhausted, Ken," she said, hoping he'd take the hint and leave her alone.

"No problem," Ken said, backing up a little and holding up his palms. "Look, I know you're upset. I just wanted you to know that you can talk to me if you need to. . . . I mean, about your parents."

Maria's whole body tensed. "Is that it?" she asked.

Ken drew back. "Well, actually, I was also going to ask you if I can get a couple of tickets for Saturday's performance," he said hesitantly. "So I can . . . come see you."

Maria closed her eyes and exhaled sharply. "You know what? Don't even bother coming," she said, holding up one hand. "I'm going to suck, and no one wants to see me anyway." She turned around and stomped back down the hall, staring at the floor all the way to avoid Tia and Jessica. *I don't even know why I came tonight,* she thought, pushing the dressing-room door so hard, it knocked against the cement wall before swinging shut again. *This whole thing is pointless.*

Maria walked over to the mirror, flopped down onto a stool, and stared at the counter. Her eyes fell on her picture from *Annie,* and her stomach turned. Slowly she looked up and down the long, impeccably organized dressing table and shook her head. Her things weren't just in the center of the counter— they were taking up half the surface.

Her friends were right. She had been acting like a snob. An intolerable, conceited snob.

Tia and Jessica walked up to Ken, who had to snap himself out of his shocked stupor.

"She belongs on soaps, not in a school play," Tia said, adjusting the top of her dress.

"What's her problem anyway?" Jessica asked, staring at the closed dressing-room door. "She's turning into one of those Hollywood actresses no one wants to work with."

"And just think," Tia said, "we can say we knew her before the fame went to her head."

"Is that the same as knowing a serial killer when he was just a quiet kid who always kept to himself?" Jessica asked with a twisted smile. Tia giggled.

"Hey, lay off," Ken said, glaring at the two girls. "It's not her fault." Both Tia and Jessica stepped back to stare at Ken.

"It's not her fault she's acting like a two-year-old?" Tia asked, lowering one eyebrow.

Ken shrugged and combed his fingers through his wavy blond hair. "I know it looks that way to you," he said, "but trust me, she's got a good reason."

Jessica tilted her head. "What do you mean?" she asked, wrinkling her nose. "What's going on?"

Ken backed off a little. "I'm not going to talk about Maria's business behind her back," he said, trying to sound diplomatic. "Besides, it's complicated." Tia and Jessica eyed him suspiciously. Ken knew they were looking for more details, but he wasn't about to supply them.

"We all have problems," Tia said, tossing her hair behind her shoulders, "but that doesn't mean we can go around acting like jerks and expecting everyone else to just deal with it."

"Well, maybe in this case it does," Ken said quietly. Jessica and Tia both looked at each other and shrugged moodily. He knew they weren't satisfied with his explanation, but there was nothing else he could say. He just hoped they'd snap out of it and try to be more understanding.

"I've got to get going," he said, turning to leave. There was no sense hanging around and waiting for Maria—there was nothing he could do for her now. *But maybe . . .* , Ken thought as he headed down the hallway, *maybe there's something I can do on my own.*

# Maria Slater

When I was eight and Nina was twelve, we were both chosen to submit projects for the statewide education fair. I did mine on ballet, complete with a five-minute solo I was scheduled to perform on the main stage at 8 P.M. sharp. I talked about it for weeks, and <u>everyone</u> knew how excited I was about performing, but when the time came, my parents weren't around—just Uncle Rudy and Aunt Jane with their video camera. They said that at the last minute, a TV crew had stopped to interview Nina about her project—a scale model of the space shuttle—and my parents had decided to stay so she wouldn't be alone.

Now here I am almost ten years later, about to be preserved on videotape again so my parents can catch Nina's performance live. I guess I shouldn't be surprised. All I know is I'm getting out of the house early tomorrow—there's no way I'm going to hang around and watch my parents take off for Nina again.

# CHAPTER
## At the Races
# 10

Ken looked around the dark, smoke-filled lounge. The yellowed walls were decorated with saddles, autographed photos of jockeys, racing shirts, and mirrors advertising various beers—but no clocks. *I should have worn my watch,* he thought. They hadn't been at the track long, but he was already starting to feel uncomfortable.

"Hey, Matthews—how's your throwing arm these days?" Will Simmons asked, punching Ken on the shoulder on his way back from the bar.

Ken tried not to roll his eyes. "All right, I guess," he answered, shrugging. *Why did Angel have to bring him?* he wondered, glancing over at Will. In a white T-shirt, a blue oxford, and khaki pants, Will was the consummate preppy jock. He had it all—the blond hair buzzed short on the sides, the angular jaw, the muscular neck, and the broad shoulders. *One look and anyone would peg him as the cocky quarterback,* Ken thought. Then he smirked. He could have just described himself a year ago.

"Just 'all right,' huh?" Will asked, raising his

151

eyebrows. "Any chance you might rejoin the team?"

Ken almost laughed. "I don't think so," he answered, looking down into his soda and fidgeting with the straw. Across the table he noticed Will's rigid features relaxing a little. It was obvious that he still considered Ken a threat when it came to football, even though Ken had no intention of getting back into it. *If I have to sit here and talk football with Will all night, I'm gonna lose it,* Ken thought, hoping someone would rescue him from the impending conversation.

"Hey—how long have we been here, man?" Angel asked, elbowing Andy to pry his attention away from the televisions simulcasting the races for lounge patrons.

Andy consulted his watch. "Twenty long minutes," he answered, dragging out each syllable. Everyone laughed except Conner.

"So what are you saying?" he demanded, searching their faces. "Are you all bored already?"

Andy waved off the question. "Not at all," he answered, his voice dripping with sarcasm. "I love watching horses. They're such noble beasts."

Conner scowled at Andy for a moment, then laughed. He turned to the others. "You guys too?" he asked with a nod. Ken shrugged, avoiding the question, and Will did the same.

Angel squirmed a little in his seat. "Well, uh . . . it was probably a lot different coming here as a kid."

"Actually," Conner said, surveying the room, "everything is pretty much the same." The table fell silent. Conner was staring at the ceiling as if he was conjuring up old memories, and everyone else seemed suddenly interested in their drinks.

*Great,* Ken thought. *Now everyone's uncomfortable. Why did I say yes to this?*

Just then Conner turned back to Angel with a challenge in his eyes. "You know, there is one thing that's different," he said.

"What's that?" Angel asked, furrowing his brow.

"Betting," Conner answered, pushing up the sleeves of his dark green, crew-neck shirt and leaning forward with his elbows on the table. He was staring at Angel with a mischievous grin.

Angel closed his eyes and shook his head. "Don't even go there, man. You know I can't."

"You don't have to," Conner answered, lifting one shoulder. "But that doesn't mean the rest of us can't."

"Uh, Conner?" Andy interrupted, raising his hand as if he were in class. "Aren't you forgetting something? We're not old enough to bet."

Conner smiled. "Angel is."

Angel cringed and rubbed his forehead with both hands. "Come on, man," he pleaded, "you just said—"

"I know what I said. *You* don't have to bet," Conner responded calmly, cutting Angel off. He leaned back in his seat and casually stretched his legs out in front of him. "You can just place bets for us," he suggested. Ken felt like he was watching a tennis match, and from where he sat, it was pretty obvious Angel was overmatched. Conner didn't seem like the kind of guy who ever took no for an answer.

"Come on, Angel," Conner continued. "You gotta admit, it'll be a lot more interesting than just sitting here. And you don't have to risk any of your own money."

Angel rolled his eyes and tipped back his head, and Ken could tell he was on the edge of giving in. He'd seen that look on a lot of football players toward the end of the game when they didn't have any fight left.

Angel looked at all of them in turn. "All right," he said finally. "I'll do it."

Conner grinned and slapped Angel on the back. He flipped quickly through the race program on their table and then pointed at one page. "I'll put five on Happy Go Lucky to win in the fourth," he said, raising his eyebrows and smirking. "Anyone else in?"

Andy's jaw went slack. "Do you even know anything about that horse?" he asked Conner.

Conner shrugged. "Don't need to," he answered matter-of-factly. "It's all in the name. That's what my dad always said."

Ken chuckled and leaned forward, taking the program from Conner. "In that case, I'll put five on So's Your Momma to show," he said.

Angel's eyes widened as he looked at Ken. "Have you done this before?" he asked.

Ken nodded and took a sip of his soda. "Once or

twice," he said. "This is my old man's lame idea of a father-son bonding experience," he added, snickering. The table went quiet, and suddenly Ken realized why. *I'm such an idiot.* "Uh, no offense, Conner," he blurted out.

"None taken," Conner responded. "So, how about you, Andy? You in?"

"I don't know," Andy said, scratching the back of his neck. "What do I have to do?"

"It's easy," Ken said. All eyes were focused on him, and he instantly regretted opening his mouth. But there was no turning back now. He cleared his throat and flipped the program around so that Andy could see it. "You just pick a horse for any race— we're looking at the fourth right now—and then decide how much to bet and whether you think your horse will win, place, or show."

Andy shot Ken a sideways glance. "Are you sure you're not some kind of Mafia horse hustler or something?"

Ken chuckled. "I've just been here a few times, that's all."

"All right," Will said, pulling his chair closer to the table. "So what's this win-place-show business all about?"

"Simple," Ken answered. "Winning, obviously, is coming in first. Placing means finishing first or second, and to show, your horse has to finish in at least third place. Get it?"

Will and Angel nodded, but Andy still looked

skeptical. "What's the smallest amount I can bet?" he asked, leaning forward a little and retrieving his wallet from the back pocket of his brown corduroys.

"Two dollars," Conner answered, standing up and reaching for his own wallet. "And I'll spot you for the first race. You too, Angel, if you're interested," he offered, removing a few bills and stuffing his wallet back in his jeans.

"I don't know," Angel hesitated.

"Hey, if Conner's paying, I'm in," Andy said, quickly scanning the program. "I'll take So's Your Momma to show too, but I'm only betting the two dollars Conner's putting up for me." He turned to Ken. "Conner's money is in your hands, buddy," he said with mock sobriety.

"Me too," Will said, nodding toward Ken as he slapped two dollars down on the table. "Let's see if you're as good at gambling as you are at football." He was smiling, but Ken couldn't help feeling like everything that came out of Will's mouth was an attempt to bait him.

Ken shook his head. "Whatever, man," he said.

Conner threw four singles into the center of the table along with Will and Ken's money. "Angel, you in?" he asked, pulling out two more dollars.

Angel hesitated, shifting in his seat. "I guess." Conner grinned and threw the bills onto the table.

"That's okay," Angel said, passing the singles back to Conner, "I'll use my own money. That way, I know I'll only bet *once*."

# TIA RAMIREZ

I CAN'T BELIEVE ANGEL HAD THE
NIGHT OFF AND DECIDED TO SPEND
IT WITH THE GUYS. WHAT HAPPENED
TO SPENDING ALL HIS FREE TIME
WITH ME? DIDN'T HE SAY THAT? I
KNOW I HEARD HIM SAY THAT.

WAIT A MINUTE. NO. I SOUND LIKE
A CLINGY, WHINY, POSSESSIVE BALL
AND CHAIN.

BUT IT STILL IRRITATES ME. WE
NEVER GET TO SEE EACH OTHER,
SO HOW IS IT SUPPOSED TO MAKE
ME FEEL WHEN HE CHOOSES THEM
OVER ME? WHEN HE GETS SOME
DOWNTIME AND WOULD RATHER
SPEND IT AT A SEEDY TRACK THAN
CUDDLE WITH ME?

AND HE CARES SO MUCH ABOUT
SAVING MONEY, RIGHT? THAT'S WHY
HE HAS TWO JOBS AND CAN NEVER
SEE ME IN THE FIRST PLACE. SO
WHAT'S HE DOING AT A PLACE

WHERE THE WHOLE POINT IS TO
THROW MONEY OUT THE WINDOW?

ALL I KNOW IS, HE'D BETTER NOT
LOSE A SINGLE DOLLAR. 'CAUSE IF
HE DOES, I'M GONNA HIT HIM SO
HARD, WHEN HE WAKES UP, HIS
CLOTHES'LL BE OUT OF STYLE.

OKAY, I'D NEVER HIT HIM. BUT
THE SENTIMENT STILL STANDS.

"Where's my horse?" Angel asked in a panicked voice as he stared at the TV monitor above his head.

Andy reached for the program in the center of the table. "What's her name again?" he asked, running his thumb down the list of horses for the last race.

"I don't remember," Angel said, turning back to the horses on the television screen, "but it's the same one Ken picked."

"Ruby Tuesday," Angel heard Ken say from the seat next to his. "She's number six." He turned to look at Ken, surprised to see him lounging back in his chair with his arms folded behind his head. *How can he be so relaxed?* Angel wondered. He spun around and desperately scanned the monitor again, but he was so nervous, he couldn't concentrate. "Where is she, Ken? How's she doing?" he asked anxiously.

"She's in second place," Ken answered calmly.

"Second?" Angel snapped, his hand landing heavily on Ken's shoulder. "But we bet on her to win, didn't we?" Suddenly he felt Will's hand on his back.

"Take it easy, Desmond," Will said, smiling. "It's just a race."

Angel looked at Will and nodded. "I know," he said, aware that he was speaking faster and louder than normal. "I know." He stared down at the table, focusing on the wet circle his soda had left on the red cloth and trying to breathe deeply. *Will's right—I have to calm down. But I bet a lot on this one,* he thought. *I could lose some serious money here.*

His first bet of the night had been a winner, and so it only made sense to bet again. After all, at that point he wasn't risking his own money anymore—just the money he had made. If he lost, he'd just be leaving with the same amount he had when he had arrived. Still, the thought of losing made him physically ill. Angel clapped a hand down on his rapidly bouncing leg.

*That fifty bucks I won could go a long way toward getting Tia something nice for our anniversary,* he thought. But if he lost, he'd be back to square one. Presentless.

"Okay, here they come," Ken announced, leaning forward to continue the play-by-play he had been giving for the races throughout the night. "They're in the stretch."

159

Angel looked back up at the screen, and his leg started bouncing involuntarily again. "Come on, Ruby," he chanted. "You can do it, baby." Angel watched as his horse moved alongside the horse in first place.

Andy gasped and elbowed Angel in the ribs. "She's passing him!" he yelled. "I can't believe it! She's passing him!"

Angel's heart was in his throat as the horses crossed the finish line. "Did she get it? Did she get it?" he asked, shaking Ken's shoulder.

Ken turned to face him and laughed. "You can relax, man," he said. "We won." He held his hand up for a high five, and Angel gladly slapped it.

"All right!" Angel yelled, practically jumping up and down. He lifted his hands in the air and cheered. Will started laughing, and when Angel spun around, he suddenly realized everyone else in the lounge was staring at him. He smiled and waved humbly, then crept back to his seat and looked at his friends, who were all grinning with obvious amusement.

"Oh, boy," Angel said, his voice quiet for the first time since the last race had begun. "I just made a pretty big scene, huh?"

Andy shook his head. "No worse than a Miss America contestant finding out she just won," he said dryly.

Angel slouched in his seat, trying to vanish. "What do you say we just collect our money and head out?" he suggested. Conner nodded and threw a few bills down on the table for the waiter, then everyone stood to go.

"So exactly how much *did* you win tonight?" Andy asked as the group moved from the lounge to the lobby.

Angel took a moment to calculate his winnings in his head. "After I pick this up," he said, nodding toward the payoff window, "I should just clear three hundred."

"Whoa!" Andy said. "And I thought I was doing good with thirty-five."

Angel grinned. "Hey, I only had fifty before the last race, but thanks to my man Ken here," he said, slapping Ken on the back, "I'm a lot richer."

Ken smiled modestly and shuffled his feet as they walked. "I was just lucky," he said.

Angel shook his head. "Whatever you say, man," he said to Ken. "All I know is that if I ever come back here, I'm bringing you along." He stepped into the line at the cash window while the other guys hung back.

"Hey, Desmond," Conner called. Angel turned around. "Do you realize that you just made more money in three hours than you would in three nights at the Riot?"

Angel snorted. "Try five nights," he called back.

"So why are you wasting your time working when you could just come here every night?" Conner jested.

161

Angel laughed. "Come on, man," he said, "you know I'm not the risk-taking type."

"I think that means that Tia wouldn't let him," Andy said, pretending to whisper but making his voice loud enough for Angel to overhear.

Angel rolled his eyes and turned back around. *He's half right,* Angel thought, moving forward with the line. *Tia wouldn't be thrilled with me going to the track every night, but there's no way she's going to be disappointed that I came today.* The thought of his winnings made Angel smile. *'Cause as of tonight, the anniversary celebration is on.*

# Ken Matthews

I used to only hang out with jocks. They were the people I spent the most time with by obligation, so they were the people I knew the best. Tonight was different. For one thing, stats, beer, and women were not the main topics of conversation.

For another, no one was trying to outbrag anyone else. And I think everyone was actually listening when everyone else was talking.

After Olivia died, I couldn't be around my friends. They suddenly seemed hollow. They made me cringe. But tonight was different. Tonight I relaxed.

I never knew there was anything else out there. Now I do.

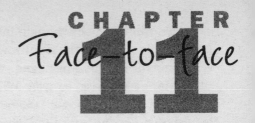
Maria peered between a small opening in the middle of the red velvet curtain. The auditorium was buzzing with conversation as parents and students filled the seats, row by row. Between the multi-colored lights shining at the stage, the deep red decor of the auditorium, and the bright attire of the bustling audience members, it almost seemed too vivid to be real.

She spotted Ned and Alice Wakefield walking down the aisle to their seats. Then she caught a glimpse of a man and a woman nudging three young boys down the aisle. The boys, all with dark hair and dark eyes, were tugging at their freshly pressed shirts and crisp ties and wincing. It was obvious they would have worn T-shirts if they had been given a choice. *It looks like Tia's mom and dad dragged her little brothers in to see her,* Maria mused, watching as the youngest rolled his eyes while his mother combed his hair into place with her fingers.

It seemed like everyone was there. *Well, not everyone,* she reminded herself. *I wonder if Nina's gotten her award yet,* she thought bitterly.

Then something in the front row caught Maria's eye. Elizabeth, Jeremy, Angel, and Andy were there, but to Maria's surprise, so were Will Simmons and Conner. *Okay,* she thought, *Conner, I understand. He's here for Tia, but still, I'm kind of shocked to see him sitting just three seats away from Liz.*

Apparently Elizabeth was too. She was sitting rigidly in her seat, staring straight forward and looking pretty pale. Maria shifted her gaze to Conner. He didn't look much better. He was just as color-free, but the fact that he was staring off into space was nothing new. Why had Maria ever thought that brooding face of his was so gorgeous? Now it just irritated her.

Then her eyes fell on Will again. He was wringing his hands and fidgeting with his jacket zipper while he talked with Angel, and he didn't look much more comfortable than Elizabeth and Conner.

Suddenly she noticed that Elizabeth, Jeremy, Andy, and Angel each had a bouquet of flowers stashed under their seats. Maria smiled.

*But why would any of them be for me?* she thought, suddenly feeling completely alone. She pulled the halves of the curtain together and stepped back. Tia and Jessica were right. She'd been nothing but a pain all week. Maria brought her hands to her face and took a deep breath as she thought over the past few days.

She didn't think she'd even talked to any of her friends except to gloat about her role or offer stupid acting advice. She was sure they all hated her by now. The thought resonated inside her until she felt nauseated. She'd been so rude to Tia and Ken yesterday afternoon. It was no wonder she hadn't heard from anyone all day.

Maria closed her eyes tight, holding back tears. *I should just leave. No one wants me here anyway.* The tears were about to spill over, but Maria held them back when she realized that she wasn't alone. Tia and Jessica had just come around the corner and were hovering nearby.

"What are you guys doing back here?" Maria asked, quickly dabbing under her heavily made-up eyes with the back of her finger.

Jessica shrugged, smiling tentatively. "We just came to wish you luck."

"Yeah, break something," Tia added, grinning.

"That's *break a leg*, Tia," Jessica corrected her.

Tia scrunched her eyes indignantly. "I know that," she said. "I just like to give people options."

"Anyway," Jessica said, "we know you're going to be fabulous. Knock 'em dead."

Maria was overwhelmed with relief. "Thanks, you guys," she said, stepping forward to hug them both at once. "After the way I've been acting this week, I wouldn't blame you if you wanted to knock *me* dead," she said with a weak smile.

Tia grinned. "Well . . . ," she said, as if considering the idea. "Maybe for a little while yesterday afternoon, but it passed."

Maria blinked, aware that tears had begun streaming down her face. "I'm sorry," she said, looking down and wiping her cheeks with the side of her hand. "Really. I've just been so tense, I guess."

"It's been a tense week," Jessica said, shrugging. "Apology accepted."

"Ditto," Tia added, smiling warmly. Then her face fell. "Okay, you've got a serious mascara crisis going on," she said, eyeing Maria's face.

"No surprise there," Maria said. "I'll go take care of it." She smiled at her friends. "You guys break a leg too."

As she walked to the dressing room, Maria realized her normal quick pace was back. *I'm going to be all right,* she told herself. *In fact, I'm going to go out there and kick butt.* So what if her parents didn't give a damn? There were other people counting on her. She pushed open the dressing-room door and headed straight for the mirror. *But you know what,* she told herself, studying her reflection, black streaks and all, *those other people don't matter either.*

Tonight she was counting on herself.

"I love this part," Jessica whispered to Tia as they watched the play from the wings.

"You mean when she says, 'If you need space, join NASA, baby'?" Tia asked.

"Yeah," Jessica answered. "I'm going to use that line the next time some guy tries to dump me. And I'm going to say it exactly the way Maria does."

Tia nodded. "She's definitely got attitude."

Jessica listened for the line, and when Maria delivered it perfectly, Jessica smiled and nudged Tia. "She really is good, isn't she?" Jessica asked.

"Mm-hmm," Tia answered. "Steady too. You'd never know how nervous she was before she went onstage."

"I just hope I can be half that stable when I have to kiss Charlie in the next scene," Jessica said.

Tia chuckled. "Speaking of kisses . . . are you excited about your date tomorrow night?"

Jessica frowned and gave Tia a little push. "I'm excited about the concert, if that's what you mean," she answered. "But it's not *my* date, remember? It's *our* date. You and Liz are going with me, you know, and I don't intend to kiss either one of you."

Tia stifled a laugh. "I meant the guy, Jessica."

"I'm not kissing him either," Jessica said indignantly. "I just plan to wait outside long enough to see who the freak is, and then we can ditch him."

"Even if he's cute?" Tia asked, glancing at Jessica out of the corner of her eye.

Jessica looked at her friend and scowled. "Even if he's Leonardo DiCaprio's twin brother."

After the second curtain call the audience's applause finally dwindled, and Maria made her way backstage. She had barely gotten to the dressing room when people started pouring in with so many bouquets of flowers that it smelled like a florist's shop.

"You were great, Maria," Alice Wakefield said, wrapping her up in a hug.

"Thank you," Maria responded.

"I agree," Ned Wakefield said as he kissed her cheek. "Jessica's been raving about you all week, but I was still impressed."

Maria was so grateful for the praise that she thought she might start crying again, but she fought to keep it together. "Wow, thank you," she said. "Jessica did a great job too." Mr. Wakefield smiled and nodded, stepping aside so the other people waiting behind him could speak with Maria.

"*Fantástico!*" Tia's mother said as she leaned in and kissed Maria's cheek. "*Qué buena actriz,*" she said, cupping Maria's chin in her hand briefly before moving along. As one person after another came up to congratulate Maria, she began to feel overwhelmed. *I don't even know half of these people,* she thought, but she continued to smile and shake hands just the same. She was as light as a cloud.

When there was a break in the throng, Maria began looking around for familiar faces. Just then someone tapped her on the shoulder.

"These are for you, Madame Slater," Andy said, bowing before her as if she were royalty.

Maria laughed. "You can get up, Andy," she said, smiling widely. She smelled the bouquet of red and white carnations he had given her. "Thank you so much," she said, hugging him. Over Andy's shoulder Maria could see Jessica standing with Jeremy, Elizabeth, and her parents. Off to the right Tia was holding her brother Tomás and laughing with Angel and the rest of her family. As Andy released her from the embrace, Maria found herself feeling suddenly sad again.

"Are you all right?" Andy asked, studying her face.

"Yeah, it's just . . ." *I wish my parents could have been here to see me tonight,* she thought. But she didn't want to whine about that to Andy. "I'm just coming down, you know? Being out there in front of everyone is such a high."

Andy nodded, but Maria noticed that he didn't look quite convinced by her explanation. "You sure?" he asked.

"Yeah, I'm fine," Maria assured him. Suddenly Andy glanced over her shoulder and smiled. Maria turned to see Ken walking toward her with a huge bouquet of roses. His hair was freshly cut, and he was wearing a button-down shirt and tie over recently ironed chinos.

To her surprise, Maria's heart instantly started pounding in her ears.

"I knew you'd be great," Ken said, handing her

171

the flowers. Maria's eyes were wide as she took in the beautiful arrangement. There had to be at least a dozen red roses tied up in lovely white silk ribbons.

"These are gorgeous!" she said, staring at Ken in disbelief. He smiled modestly and looked down at his feet, but Maria wasn't going to let him just shrug it off. She shifted Ken's flowers into her left arm with the flowers Andy had just given her and then wrapped her right arm around his shoulders. "Thank you, Ken. This is really sweet."

Ken stepped back a little, and Maria saw that he was blushing. He met her eyes briefly, then looked down and coughed into his hand, clearing his throat. "I have something else for you too," he said, looking over his shoulder and waving at someone.

Ken stepped aside, allowing Maria to view the crowd behind him, and her jaw dropped.

"Dad?" she gasped, staring in disbelief.

Jack Slater walked over to his daughter and threw his arms around her. "You were wonderful, sweetheart," he whispered in her ear. "I knew you would be."

Maria handed her flowers to Ken and hugged her father tightly with both arms, hardly able to believe he was really there.

"But what a-about . . . ?" Maria stammered. She shook her head and let her voice trail off, so shocked by her father's sudden appearance that she was unable to formulate the complete sentence.

Maria's father smiled at her, his eyes full of compassion. "After you blew up at us yesterday, your mother and I rethought things, and we decided to split up for the weekend. And this young man," he said, pulling Ken closer, "was kind enough not only to get me a ticket, but also to persuade the man taping for the school to make an extra copy of the video for your mother."

Maria's heart fluttered. She grinned at Ken and shook her head. "You're amazing," she told him, but Ken just shuffled his feet and looked away. "But Dad," she said, turning back to her father. "Aren't you kind of sorry you missed Nina's big scholarship thing?"

Mr. Slater shrugged. "Your mother's videotaping," he said, to Maria's delight. "And besides, once I realized how important this was to you, there was no way I was going to miss it."

Maria felt another tear slide down her cheek. *I'm turning into a fountain,* she thought, accepting a handkerchief from her father and dabbing at her eyes for what seemed like the twentieth time that night.

"I only wish you'd told me sooner how much this play meant to you," Mr. Slater continued, pulling something from his jacket pocket. "Then I wouldn't be stuck with this nonrefundable airline ticket." He smiled and touched the ticket gently to her forehead.

Maria laughed and hugged her father, starting to

cry all over again. *My mascara is probably streaked down to my chin,* she thought, but somehow this time it didn't seem to matter.

"There he is!" Tia said, pointing excitedly. Jessica followed the direction of Tia's gesture and saw a man who had to be at least seventy. He had a long white beard, and he was walking with a cane.

"Very funny." Jessica scowled. "But I don't think Uncle Sam is my secret admirer." Tia laughed and continued to scan the crowd outside the coliseum, where the concert was taking place. There were a ton of people making their way through the entrance, and Jessica had even seen a few cute guys, but so far no one had approached her, claiming to be her stalker.

"Ooh! How about that guy?" Elizabeth said, pointing at a man about thirty feet away. He was probably in his twenties, and he wasn't bad looking, but as he got closer, Jessica realized that what she had thought were black jeans were really leather pants. Actually, everything the guy was wearing was made of leather, including his tight-fitting vest. And although it had looked like he was wearing a color-ful, long-sleeved shirt from a distance, his arms were actually covered with tattoos.

Jessica glared at her sister and Tia, who seemed to be beside themselves with laughter. "Are you guys going to point out *every* freak we see and claim he's my secret admirer?" she demanded.

"Of course not," Tia responded seriously. "There are way too many for us to point out all of them." Elizabeth laughed, but Jessica just rolled her eyes. She didn't know why she had let them come. In fact, she was beginning to wonder why she had come herself. But inside, Jessica knew that the idea of meeting her so-called secret admirer intrigued her. Actually, it positively excited her. Otherwise she wouldn't have spent an entire day choosing an outfit and two hours getting ready.

*I'm just going to ignore them,* Jessica thought, tuning out her sister and Tia as she straightened the cashmere vest she had secretly borrowed from Lila's closet. *Lila owes me this much after all the crap she's done,* Jessica thought, admiring how crisp the red vest looked against her simple white T-shirt and black linen miniskirt. All she needed now was for the guy to show up.

"Um, Jess?" she heard Elizabeth say warily, while Tia simultaneously nudged her with an elbow.

Jessica lifted her head and immediately knew what—or rather *who*—they were looking at. She stared for a moment, aware that she was wide-eyed and slack jawed, but she couldn't seem to move.

Will Simmons stood in front of her, smiling and shifting nervously on his feet. "Hey," he said, pointing to the two slips of paper she had just dropped on the ground. "I see you got the tickets."

# WILL SIMMONS
## 7:43 P.M.

<u>Note</u> <u>to</u> <u>self</u>:

Secret-admirer thing? Not the best idea.

I only did it because I knew Melissa would freak out if she saw me actually hanging around with Jessica. And I had a feeling Jessica would, you know, push me away or whatever if I tried to ask her out directly.

Maybe I should have come up with my own poems or something. But if there's one thing I don't have confidence in, it's my own writing ability. Anything I came up with would probably sound like Dr. Seuss.

Only not as good.

I don't know. I was just hoping. . . .

I don't know.

I just want to be with her.

# JESSICA WAKEFIELD

## 7:43 P.M.

Oh . . . my . . . God.

# JEREMY AAMES

## 7:43 P.M.

*The money came through. My dad has a job. We just found out, and I can't wait to tell Jessica.*

*I wonder what she's doing right now.*